" . . . An impressive compilation . . . "
*The Irish Times*

Praise for **CHILLER**

"These haunting tales are for reading by the fireside. The sensually eerie cover is by PJ Lynch."
*The Sunday Tribune*

"A wide range of themes, from wistful ghost stories to horrifying tales of the undead, will please even the most reluctant reader."
*Children's Book Festival Reading List 1996-1997*

"Wonderfully spooky cover by PJ Lynch."
*Children's Book Festival Reading List 1996-1997*

And don't miss

**NIGHTMARES**

Terrifying tales from beyond the grave . . .

# SHIVER!

*Fifteen ghostly stories from some of
Ireland's best writers*

**POOLBEG**

*Editor's Note*

Special thanks to MS for thinking of the title!

Published in 1994 by
Poolbeg Press Ltd
123 Baldoyle Industrial Estate
Dublin 13, Ireland

Reprinted November 1996

The moral right of the authors has been asserted.

A catalogue record for this book is available from the British Library.

ISBN 1 85371 300 7

Cover illustration by PJ Lynch
Cover design by Poolbeg Group Services Ltd
Set by Poolbeg Group Services Ltd in Goudy 11.5/14
Printed by The Guernsey Press Company Ltd,
Vale, Guernsey, Channel Islands.

# CONTENTS

# THE BLACK DOLL
*Rose Doyle*

I got a letter this morning from my Aunt Tess. She was
in New Zealand when she wrote it but was getting
ready to move on. My Aunt Tess is an anthropologist
and travels a lot.

For a long time, when I was younger, I thought I'd be
an anthropologist too. I liked the idea of spending my
time in hot, exotic countries, wearing a white safari hat
as I went around investigating how the people there
lived. I stopped thinking about a career in anthropology
a year ago. Something happened then which made me
think that training tigers, or even becoming an
astronaut, might be safer things to do with my life.

It's not that I'm forever brooding about what
happened. There are days now when I don't think about
it at all. And even when it *does* pop into my head I
don't shake all over, the way I used to do for a long time
afterwards.

But Aunt Tess's letter brought it all back with a rush.
Reading it I could see her at work, imagine her

examining her specimens . . . And the terrible events of that October night might have happened yesterday.

My grandmother died last year too. For years and years she lived alone in this house, the one my family and I live in now. It's a big house, in an old part of Dublin, and it's right beside a small graveyard.

When my grandmother was alive we lived in the country. We used to spend part of every summer here and we always had a terrific time. This was mostly because my grandmother was really good fun and used to take myself and my two young brothers to all sorts of interesting places. She died in the spring, so of course we didn't come for a holiday last summer. It was a miserable summer. It rained a lot too. I was feeling pretty fed up when, one day in August, my mother came into my room.

"I want to talk to you, Niamh," she patted a spot on the bed and I slid down beside her, warily. Calling me by my full name was a bad sign. I've been called Nim for as long as I can remember.

"Niamh . . . " She took a deep breath and I squirmed. "We're moving to Dublin. Your grandmother has left me the house in her will. It'll be a few months before Dad and myself and the boys are ready to leave but we've decided that you should go on ahead and get started in your new school . . . "

I thought she was joking at first. Then I saw in her face that she wasn't.

"You mean I'm to live in the house on my own?" All I could think of was how empty it would be without Grandmother.

"Of course not." My mother gave me a breath-squeezing hug. "Your Aunt Tess will look after you. She'll be doing some research work."

Aunt Tess came for me at the end of the month.

"My, but you've grown!" she said as she hurried me to her car. I was exactly the same size as when she'd seen me six months before but I said nothing. She drove fast and talked about anthropology all the way to Dublin.

"I've made a bed for you in the room you usually sleep in." She had hardly closed the front door before she started up the stairs with my suitcase.

I followed her, looking around as I went. I had expected the house to be different, somehow, but it was just the same. It wasn't dusty, or cold. It didn't even feel empty. It was the same dark, old-fashioned house it had always been.

My room was at the back and by the time I got there Aunt Tess had thrown open the window.

"We need some fresh air in here," she held out her hand and I went and stood beside her. She put an arm around me. "Your own private graveyard view!" She laughed. "I hope it doesn't bother you . . . "

Her laugh seemed to hang in the air outside.

Aunt Tess didn't understand about me and the graveyard. It didn't bother me at all. The view of the headstones and grass was far nicer than the traffic-filled street you could see from the front of the house. The colours too, green and grey, were the ones I was used to from the stone-filled fields at home. And I liked the old tree under my window as well, the way its branches shaded both my grandmother's garden and the graveyard.

"I like it," I said.

Aunt Tess left me to unpack. After I'd stuffed the last of my things into drawers I went back to the window. The graveyard had been there a long time. Longer than most of the houses even. There were only twelve graves and I knew by heart the names on all the stones. Sometimes, on summer evenings, Grandmother and I used to walk around them. She knew about the lives of all the people buried there.

"We're taking a stroll through history," she said once. "Every one of these graves has a bit of what made this area buried in it . . . "

Standing by the window that day I could almost hear her.

But the voice calling me up the stairs belonged most definitely to Aunt Tess.

"Orla's here! Come on down and say hello."

Orla lives next door. She's a year younger than me but behaves as if she's ten years older. This is because she believes that living in the city automatically makes people more intelligent. I had already tried to sort her out on this one but she's slow to learn. Still, in the weeks which followed she was a good friend. She helped me find my way around the school, which seemed really huge to me at first, and she walked there and back with me every day.

I didn't see very much of Aunt Tess. She'd turned the dining-room into a study and spent most of her time working in there. It wasn't a bit like living in the house with Grandmother and I became aware of things I'd never even noticed before. Like how the traffic never stopped at night and the way the lights never went out. I missed the soft, evening darkness of the countryside and the quiet silence that put me to sleep every night.

I had been living with Aunt Tess for a month when the box arrived. I was on my way out to school when she opened the door to the delivery man.

"At last!" She clapped her hands and almost screeched. It was a big box, covered in foreign-looking markings. After the man left she danced around it in the dining-room. I hovered a bit but she shooed me off to school. "Off you go," she said, "or you'll be late. You can see them when you get home."

I went, slowly. The arrival of the box was the only interesting thing which had happened in the whole month. I wondered all day what could be in it, what Aunt Tess had meant by 'them'. If I'd known then what I know now I wouldn't have gone home after school that day. I'd have found some way of staying away until she'd sent the contents of the box back where they belonged.

But I didn't know and so I couldn't wait for school to end. I even boasted about the box to Orla. She was dead interested.

"Can I come in and see what's in it?" she asked. "Maybe it's full of snake skins. Or shrunken skulls from the forests of Borneo . . . "

"Don't be stupid," I said.

But Orla wasn't so very far wrong.

Aunt Tess had lined up the contents of the box on the dining-room mantelpiece. We saw them as soon as we came in.

"Ugh!" Orla said and began to giggle. I just stared. The back of my neck prickled and my mouth went dry. I moved closer.

"What are they?" Orla reached to touch one.

"Voodoo dolls," I said.

"Quite right, Nim." Aunt Tess had come into the room. "How did you know that?"

"Guessed," I said. But I hadn't. I'd just known, somehow, that the six, grotesque, wooden figures were voodoo dolls.

"They come from the Caribbean," Aunt Tess touched one fondly. "They're very old, very precious specimens. You'll never see any others like them."

"I never want to . . . " I muttered, but under my breath. I could see that she thought a lot of them. The minute I'd seen them I'd felt they were unlucky, or bad somehow. One doll in particular scared me. It was a man dressed all in black. His eyelids drooped over a pair of inky, glittering eyes and he had a sneering half-smile. All the dolls were ugly but he was sinister as well. He made the others look like Barbies.

"What are voodoo dolls?" Orla asked.

I moved away quickly as Aunt Tess lifted down the black doll. She touched its eyes with the tip of her finger. "They're part of the voodoo religion. They're said to have all sorts of powers."

"I remember," Orla said excitedly, "if you stick pins in them you can make people sick . . . "

"Well, yes, that's one of the ways they're used . . . "

"Aunt Tess, do *you* believe they have powers?" I asked.

"It depends," she smiled.

I hate it when adults answer like that. "Depends on what?" I was quite rude.

"On where I am . . . " She put the black doll on the

6

table and sat looking at it. She seemed to have forgotten all about us. Orla made a face at me and we backed out of the room.

"What a yucky, ugly-looking bunch . . . " She wrinkled her nose and helped herself to some biscuits in the kitchen. I was thinking that I didn't want to live in the house with the black doll. It was such a stupid idea that I didn't say anything out loud.

After a while Orla went home to do her homework. I sat down to do my own but found I was still shivering. I heated some milk in the microwave, wishing that my mother was there. Or even that she would telephone. I closed my eyes and prayed for the phone to ring but nothing happened.

Aunt Tess worked in the dining-room all evening. I knocked on the door as I was going to bed but she didn't answer. Sometimes she came up after me to say goodnight but that night she didn't.

I suppose she thought that at twelve years old I was a bit big to need someone saying goodnight to me all the time.

I lay down and tried not to think about the voodoo doll downstairs, to forget his black, unblinking eyes. But every time I thought I'd put him out of my head he popped up again, smiling at me from the darkness beyond my eyelids.

The shivers I'd had earlier had gone and I was feeling hot now instead. I got out of bed, pulled back the curtains and opened the window a little. The graveyard was peaceful as ever. There was a full moon and the gravel path shone silver, the headstones throwing shadows across it. A small wind shook the tree by my window and the branches beckoned to me. I watched them waving and knew, in that moment, that the black voodoo doll had somewhere, and in another time, done a great evil.

Leaving the window open I got back into bed. I propped myself up with a pile of pillows and, looking out at the graveyard and remembering walks there with my grandmother, I fell asleep at last.

I don't know how long I'd been asleep before the sounds woke me. I thought it was morning until I saw that the moon was shining right across my bed. The sounds really came to me when I sat up. First there was a wild chanting, then the terrible cries of people wailing. I covered my ears but they didn't go away. A drum began to pound somewhere in the background and I froze, rigid with fear as it started up the stairs. I couldn't understand why Aunt Tess didn't seem to hear it. Maybe, like me, she was lying petrified in her bed. I tried to call out but couldn't even manage a whisper. The chanting grew louder. The groans became terrified pleading. The drum beat faster. Suddenly, it all stopped and there was a shocking silence.

I turned my head toward the door just as a dark shape slipped through it. I knew it was the doll. I held my breath, hoping that if I gave no sign of life he might go away. He didn't. I couldn't see him any more, and he made no sound. But I knew he was still in the room. I could feel his evil all around me.

I looked, very slowly, toward the window. I was wondering if I could escape that way. But the doll had thought of that too. He was standing beside the window now. Two greeny points of light shone from his eyes and caught my gaze. I couldn't move my eyes away. I wanted to scream, jump out of bed. I couldn't do anything.

Then the doll did a strange thing. It raised one of its stiff, wooden arms and pointed down toward the graveyard. As it did so its eyes flickered and I was freed.

I was out of bed and halfway to the door before I realised the doll had got there before me. Its smile was more sinister than ever and I backed away, around the bed and toward the window again. The doll kept coming. Its eyes caught mine once more and the greeny light got brighter and brighter.

I felt the air from the window behind me and knew I could go no further unless I jumped. The doll touched me.

It was a city sound which saved me in the end. An ambulance started up shrill and loud above the other night noises. I started and freed myself again from the doll's eyes. I felt it move away and knew that it was trying to catch my gaze again. But I didn't look down, not even when I felt it close in against me, scratchy and wooden.

Instead I turned and looked out the window, down at the graveyard. The wind was stronger now and the branches of the old tree beckoned for the second time that night.

This time I paid attention. Closing my eyes I bent down. In one quick, fierce movement I caught the doll in both my hands and threw it, as hard as I could, into the branches of the tree. I opened my eyes to see the branches toss it down, down between them into the graveyard. It lay, spread-eagled on a grave, a dark shape with pins of light still coming from where its eyes were.

I couldn't stop shivering. I found my dressing-gown, then my slippers. As I put them on I knew I couldn't leave the doll where it was. It wouldn't be right. It should have a grave of its own. And if it were buried down there it would do no more harm. The peaceful dead of the graveyard would see to that.

I found a shovel in the kitchen and crossed the garden into the graveyard. I knew exactly where the branches had thrown the doll and I didn't feel a bit afraid now. I would be protected.

A cloud crossed the moon and at first I thought this was why I couldn't find the doll. But when the moon came out again I could see, quite clearly, that there was nothing on the grave. I searched the one beside it, then the next one. I searched all twelve graves but I didn't find the doll.

It was almost dawn when Aunt Tess found me, huddled by a headstone. I woke when she tried to lift me up.

"Oh, Nim, what are you doing here?" Her face, bending over me, was very white. And worried. "Are you all right?"

"I'm fine," I said and to prove it I got to my feet on my own.

Aunt Tess put an arm around me and we went slowly back to the house. Before we went indoors I managed a last sneaky look around, there was no sign anywhere of the doll.

Aunt Tess insisted on getting the doctor to make sure I wasn't suffering from exposure or anything. She fussed about an awful lot, telling me how she'd discovered my bedroom door open and gone in to find I wasn't there. The open kitchen door had led her to the graveyard.

The doctor was quite old. He'd known my grandmother and we chatted about her for a while. Then he asked me why I'd been sleeping in the graveyard. I told him everything, exactly as I'd already told Aunt Tess. He patted my hand when I'd finished and I could tell he didn't believe me.

"When do the rest of the family arrive?" he asked Aunt Tess.

"Not for another ten days," she was still pale and shaky-looking. Not that I blamed her.

"Keep her home for the rest of the week," the doctor was brisk. "Feed her up, keep her warm and see she has plenty of rest."

They left the room, talking together as if I wasn't there. When they stopped on the landing I put an ear to the door to listen.

"She's obviously had a bad nightmare," the doctor was saying. "Brought on by the fact that she's missing her grandmother and separated from the rest of the family. She'll be fine once they get here."

"I'm sure you're right," Aunt Tess said.

So she didn't believe me either! Wait until she goes to look for the black doll . . .

"Sleeping in that room doesn't help, of course . . . " The doctor's voice faded as they went down the stairs and all I heard was 'graveyard' and 'imagination'.

I got back into bed and buried myself under the clothes. It had *not* been a nightmare. I closed my eyes and it all came back to me, stark as the night before. I could see the pins of green light, glowing . . .

I opened my eyes and sat up. I was concentrating on the reality of a whole week off school when Aunt Tess came back into the room.

"Feeling better?" She sat on the bed. I thought she looked pretty awful herself but I said nothing. She took my hand. Hers was very cold.

"What did you do with the black doll, Nim? It's very valuable, you know . . . "

"I threw it out the window and it disappeared from the grave. I told you . . . "

She got up, went to the window and stood looking at the graveyard for a while. When she came back she hugged me tight and I held on to her.

"You're all right, Nim, that's the main thing," she said.

I knew then that Aunt Tess believed me. When I came downstairs later in the day she'd packed the other five dolls into the box, ready to be sent away. The black doll wasn't there and she never again asked me about it.

# ABSENT-MINDED IVAN
## Gretta Mulrooney

Picture poor Ruairi Dooley. He was sitting with Bag O'Bones by the trapdoor of a castle dungeon and he was rottenly, horribly, absolutely miserable. He was so miserable, he didn't even smile when Bag O'Bones sat up and begged with her head on one side. Bag O'Bones grumbled, gave up and lay down. No doggie treats today.

Ruairi had been abandoned in a damp-smelling castle by his parents, who had gone off to visit his eldest sister in England. His uncle Johnny owned the castle. It was perched on the borders of Tipperary and Limerick. Johnny had made his fortune from buying and selling Russian army weapons and bits of the Berlin wall. A Soviet army tank sat outside by the castle moat like a gloomy sentry.

"Ruairi will be fine," Johnny had told his parents, "he'll have the twins to play with all day long. They'll get on like a house on fire!" Ruairi cuddled up to Bag O'Bones. "I'm glad you're here," he whispered in her ear, "at least you talk to me. The twins!" He snorted and the dog quivered and pushed her warm nose into Ruairi's neck.

The twins. Peas in a pod. Johnny's sons, Kieran and Tommy. It wasn't that the twins were nasty to him. They ignored him. Ruairi would have preferred arguments or falling out. The twins were polite, except for the odd time when they made up names. If they found him reading they called him, 'Ruairi Schooley'. When he dropped Uncle Johnny's musket they called him 'Ruairi Fooley'.

The twins had lived in America and all over Europe. They were best friends, they didn't need anyone else. They especially didn't need someone who preferred reading and drawing to shooting and archery and model weapons. The twins shared their father's fascination with military things. They loved magazines about war, submarines, guns, missiles. They talked about things like, 'the best way to camouflage a tank', or, 'how to survive in hand-to-hand combat'. In the shed was a rifle range where they practised every morning. In the afternoons they helped Johnny clean guns. Ruairi hated them. He hated their army stuff and loud voices and their big feet and the way they jumped on each other in mock fights. Ruairi was a pacifist. He would have refused to fight if there was a war. He'd rather go to jail than kill anyone. He wished that his parents had left him in his own house in Wexford where he had his modelling clay and paint-brushes. But he was only twelve, too young to be 'home alone'.

Kieran and Tommy came crashing through the door waving machineguns. When they saw him they stopped and Kieran said something that sounded like, 'egz vitch hoken brodski'. It could have been any language, they knew so many and they often spoke in one of them when Ruairi was around. Ruairi felt as if he was full of poison. When they'd gone he banged the rim of the trapdoor. Uncle Johnny had told him that unwanted visitors at the castle used to fall through it into a vat of boiling oil.

"If there was boiling oil down there," he told Bag O'Bones, "I'd drop the trapdoor when they ran in."

As soon as he said it he felt terrible. Him, a pacifist, planning to deep-fry his cousins!

That night Ruairi was sitting in his room, staring into his mirror. He was practising drawing himself. His face was pale and pinched and his mouth was turned down. A breeze suddenly brushed the back of his neck.

"In Moscow we have a saying," a thin voice said, "'his look would pickle cabbage.'"

There was a face by his left shoulder, a bony face topped by cropped hair. Ruairi swallowed. He kept looking in the mirror.

"You are thinking, what is this? A ghost? You're right, I am."

Ruairi turned round slowly. He put his hands on his knees to stop them trembling. The ghost moved to the window. He was a young man, tall, wearing a uniform of brown trousers and jacket. The trousers were tucked into muddy boots. From outside came the noise of Uncle Johnny scraping rust from the tank and the echo of 'ack-ack-ack-ack' as the twins pretended to fire its gun. Uncle Johnny had said there would certainly be ghosts in the castle. Someone had once seen a monk in the old chapel. No one had mentioned a Russian ghost. Were ghosts able to travel? Ruairi had never thought about it.

15

The ghost saluted. "Ivan Petrushkov, late of the Soviet army." He gave a graceful bow.

"I'm Ruairi Dooley, presently of Wexford, guest at the castle. Unwanted guest."

The ghost nodded. "Yes, I have noticed. The warlike twins. May I sit on your bed?"

"Please." Ruairi pushed books aside to make room. There are so many things I don't know about ghosts, he thought, like whether they need to sit and eat and sleep. "Would you like some Coca-Cola?" he offered.

Ivan's eyes widened. "Yes! You could only get it on the black market in Moscow." He guzzled the bottle Ruairi gave him and burped loudly. "It's gone up my nose!" He took out a mucky hanky and blew loudly. "Now," he said, business-like, "why did you call me?"

"Sorry?" Ruairi was astonished.

"You called me. What for?"

"There must be a mistake, I didn't even know you existed . . . well, you don't exist . . . you know what I mean."

Ivan tutted and knocked his heels together. "This is complicated," he said tetchily, "I thought you must have found the wallet."

"Wallet? What wallet?"

"The wallet I've been looking for."

"I don't understand," said Ruairi. He wished he did, because Ivan had started to look very tired. Ruairi had recently studied the circulatory system at school. He wondered if a ghost had blood and if so whether Ivan's blood sugar might be low.

"Chocolate?" he offered.

Ivan perked up. "What sort?"

"Smooth, milky, little squares."

"Yes please. I haven't had anything sweet for ages."

Ruairi watched Ivan munching with a dreamy expression on his face. A gong sounded from downstairs. "Supper!" shouted Johnny. Ivan wiped his fingers.

"Best if I go now. Meet me tomorrow in the old grain store, 10 o'clock."

"Before you go," said Ruairi hastily, "where exactly have you come from?"

"Afghanistan. The journey was exhausting, bumps and rough seas. Your uncle caused me a lot of bother by buying my tank."

He vanished. The gong sounded again. Downstairs the twins were watching a video about galactic battles and munching peanut butter sandwiches.

Tommy muttered to Kieran, "luftz shizzle nontropse."

Ruairi ate an apple and was lost in thought about Ivan. He didn't notice that the twins hadn't offered him a sandwich.

In the morning Uncle Johnny made breakfast and asked Ruairi if he'd like to join in shooting practice. He asked this every morning and always looked disappointed when Ruairi said no. Usually, Ruairi slipped away after helping with the washing-up, feeling lonely and uncomfortable. This morning, though, he hummed as he made his bed and thought of the questions he wanted to ask Ivan. He'd written them down to make sure he didn't forget any:

Do you need sleep?

Are there other ghosts in the castle?

How do you vanish?

Are you happy?
Can you get flu?
Will you ever stop being a ghost?
Why do you speak English?

He got to the grain store dead on time. Ivan was already there and talking to himself with his eyes closed. "A bedroom . . . no . . . maybe the cupboard under the stairs . . . no . . . perhaps under a floorboard . . . no . . . " He opened his eyes and saw Ruairi. "It's no good, I just can't remember where I put it. I cracked my head when the bullet got me, I think it's made my memory even worse. To be honest, I was always absent-minded. I nearly forgot where I'd said I'd meet you today. When I was a soldier, I often forgot to load my rifle." He leaned forward, lowering his voice. "Between you and me, I hated the army. I can't stand fighting. You know, I'd give anything for some salted herrings."

Ruairi dug into his pocket. "I can't manage herring, but I brought more chocolate. Why did you join the army?"

Ivan munched. "No choice, I had to."

Ruairi listened, fascinated, while Ivan told him how he was swept into the army and sent to Afghanistan. He was killed two months after his eighteenth birthday. He had left the book he was reading propped on the tank turret. When he leaned out to get it a stray bullet caught him in the chest. It was just the kind of thing Ruairi could imagine doing himself.

"Maybe I put it in a book!" Ivan said suddenly. "Can you help me look through all the books in the castle?"

"Look for what?"

18

"The wallet, I told you all about it yesterday."

"No, you didn't. You only mentioned it."

"You sure?"

"Positive. I've a good memory for detail, it's because I draw."

"You see! I've a head like a sieve!" Ivan smacked at himself in annoyance, pulling faces.

Ruairi laughed. It was the first time he'd laughed in a fortnight and it felt wonderful.

Ivan started to chuckle too. Bag O'Bones raced in to see what the noise was about, skidded to a halt, looked around and stared at Ruairi as if to say, "have you gone completely raving mad?"

"Poor doggie," said Ivan, "she can't see me. I had a dog in Moscow, called Rosa. She was forgetful, like me. She used to lose her way home."

Ruairi could see that Ivan was getting dreamy again. "The wallet," he said quickly, motioning Bag O'Bones to sit, "tell me about it."

Ivan popped the last bit of chocolate in his mouth. Bag O'Bones sniffed the air suspiciously and thumped her tail.

"When I was in Afghanistan," said Ivan, "I wrote a letter for my family in case I was killed and tucked it in my wallet. I put the wallet in such a safe place that when I died no one found it. I couldn't rest without my family getting my last message so I came back to look for it. At first it was hard to trace the tank because your uncle had bought it and I had to follow it from Afghanistan. You won't be surprised to hear that when I finally got here I couldn't remember where I'd hidden the wallet. It took me days to find it, taped under the driver's seat. I removed it in case your uncle discovered it and hid it in the castle in a tearing hurry because I had to report back."

"What do you mean, report back?"

"Hmm? Oh, it's just a thing ghosts have to do now and again. Then I came back and of course I couldn't find it. I'm very good at thinking up secret places but useless at remembering them. It's been exhausting." He yawned, rubbing his eyes.

"And you thought I'd found it?" prompted Ruairi.

"Yes, because you called me."

"I didn't call you."

Ivan just smiled. "I need your help, anyway. Will you search with me? Two heads are better than one, especially when one's mine!" Ivan sounded sad. "I'm hopeless, aren't I? There's my poor mum and dad with nothing to remember me by and I'm stuck in Ireland like an idiot."

"I think your head's fine," said Ruairi firmly. "I admire you for not liking war and soldiers and all that horrible stuff. I think it's really nice of you to want to help your family. Let's start looking right now. We'll go from top to bottom." He felt full of energy and not a bit poisonous. He hadn't thought about boiling oil for hours.

Ivan leapt to his feet and did a few Cossack-type dance steps. His boots rang on the cobbled floor. Bag O'Bones growled softly and darted away to hide in the hedge.

For four days they searched high and low, from the castle ramparts to the cellars. Alcoves, cupboards, bookshelves, mattresses, wardrobes – they investigated them all. Ruairi tried to move around carefully and not draw attention to his activities. On the second day the twins found him with his hand behind a toilet pipe.

"Ahm," he said, "I'm just taking measurements to make a model of the castle."

"Ruairi Pecuerly," he heard them laugh as they ran off, but he didn't mind. He'd almost forgotten about the twins because he was so absorbed in the wallet hunt. Every morning he was up with the lark, eager to get started.

By the fourth night Ivan was fed up. He sat in Ruairi's room, eating gherkins and saying that it was hopeless. All they'd found were cobwebs and dust. They'd been sneezing so much, they'd got headaches.

"Try to remember," urged Ruairi for the hundredth time. "Where were you when you hid it?"

"It's no good, I can't think straight."

Bag O'Bones trotted in looking for fun and pulled at Ruairi's sleeve.

"Silly old dog," he told her, "what are you doing up? You're usually in bed by now."

"That's it!" Ivan leapt to his feet, clapping his hands. "That's it! It's in the kitchen. I slid it under the rush matting by the dog's basket!"

They ran down to the kitchen, tripping each other on the winding stone steps. Unfortunately, Johnny and the twins were sitting at the table, cleaning swords and eating crisps. Ruairi pretended to be interested while Ivan tried to manoeuvre his way around Bag O'Bones, who had settled down in her basket. She barked suspiciously when Ivan stretched out his hand. Ivan gestured to Ruairi to get rid of the others.

"I can't," he mouthed back and the twins stared.

"Eggzlonsk quetzy magollot ingrestfer," said Kieran.

Tommy agreed. "Oglon frettigrot humplings drotspik."

Ivan sidled up to Ruairi. "They say you're very odd but they wish that they could draw as well as you."

"How do you know?"

"I just do. Ghosts speak every language."

Ruairi gave this some thought. "I could give you drawing lessons if you like," he said to the astonished twins.

Their faces turned bright red.

"Have you been able to understand us all the time?" asked Tommy, not looking Ruairi in the eye.

"Oh yes." Ruairi was enjoying himself. "I could do the first lesson tomorrow."

"Wow!" Kieran went back to polishing but he sneaked glances at Tommy and Ruairi.

After a silence the twins said, "OK!" simultaneously. They both kept giving Ruairi careful looks.

"We won't be drawing anything to do with wars or fighting," warned Ruairi.

"No, all right," they agreed meekly.

Uncle Johnny looked at the clock. "Bedtime, everyone!"

"I'll be up in a minute," said Ruairi, "I'll just have a glass of milk."

As soon as they'd gone, he and Ivan made for Bag O'Bones's basket and Ruairi stroked her while Ivan burrowed under the mat.

"Ah," he said, "here!" He pulled out a dark leather wallet and eagerly opened it to check that a folded piece of paper was still inside. "Now I can rest easy and my parents can share the thoughts I wanted to leave them. Thank you, Ruairi."

"I didn't do that much," said Ruairi, "you remembered it yourself in the end."

"No. I'd have given up without your encouragement. You kept me going, pepped me up." Ivan leaned forward and kissed Ruairi on both cheeks, Russian-style.

The next day, Ruairi posted a wallet containing a letter to the Petrushkov family, Okholski Square, Moscow. With the letter was a note, dictated in Russian by Ivan, explaining that the wallet had been found in Ireland.

Kieran and Tommy were waiting for him when he got back from the village, pencils and sketch pads at the ready. Uncle Johnny had been left to do rifle practice on his own.

Ruairi hurried upstairs for his sketch book and a farewell. Ivan was cleaning his boots with his hanky.

"All done?" he asked.

Ruairi nodded. "It's safely posted."

Ivan sighed with relief. I'm off now then," he said. "We won't meet again."

They shook hands and smiled.

"Tell me," said Ruairi, "did you call me or did I call you?"

"That's an interesting question," Ivan said, and vanished.

Tommy shouted, "Come on, Ruairi Da Vinci Dooley! We want to get started!"

On his way downstairs, Ruairi realised that he'd never asked Ivan his list of questions. Now he'd never know if a ghost could get flu.

# ALL FALL DOWN
*Michael Carroll*

Every night I dream about that house, and I know that I will continue to do so for the rest of my life, but even now I'm not certain if what happened was real, or just a product of my vivid, youthful imagination.

I was only twelve years old then, but I knew how to look after myself. I'd been in the Scouts since I was six, and thought I knew all there was about camping and living rough.

But it's one thing to spend a warm summer evening sitting around a huge campfire with forty or more scouts of your own age, singing songs and playing games and telling jokes . . . It's quite another thing to find yourself in the ruins of an old house, the sagging roof barely sufficient to keep out the howling, freezing wind, while you huddle around a tiny fire made from the few pieces of dry timber you managed to find.

The house was pretty big. I guessed that in its day – maybe three hundred years ago – it was owned by some extremely rich family. It was probably magnificent and full of life and laughter. Now, it was a half-destroyed wreck. Many of the upper floors had collapsed completely, leaving the rotten stubs of thick beams protruding from the walls. All of the windows were broken, though I remember thinking that this was more likely due to the rotting window frames than vandalism.

And so I sat there, crouched in the corner, carefully feeding tiny pieces of wood into the fire, wondering how I could have been so stupid as to think I was able to look after myself.

I was prepared, all right. I had lots of food, a one-man tent, a small gas fire and a sleeping bag in my rucksack. The only trouble was, I didn't have my rucksack with me. I'd actually been stupid enough to put it down in the woods when I went to search for firewood. Then I came across the house, and spent a good hour or more exploring it, pretending I was rescuing a kidnapped child, that sort of thing.

It was a great house, in the daylight. From a distance, it looked almost as though someone was still living there, but as I approached, I could see that it was long abandoned. It never occurred to me to wonder why.

The house was situated in what had once been a garden, right in the middle of the woods. If there had ever been a path leading up to it, it was long overgrown. Ivy grew thick on the walls, even growing through the windows and into the upstairs rooms, and in one place the ivy had broken through the slates on the roof and appeared to be creeping towards the chimney stack.

The front door was wide open, and I just marched straight in. If I had *known* then, I would have fled from the house. But I didn't know. I was just a curious young boy, eager to explore this wonderful house.

Inside, a half-demolished staircase wound its way up to the first and second floors. With difficulty, I managed to climb up, and began to explore the rooms.

The first room had once been a bedroom – I guessed this because, while there was no longer a bed in the room, there was an ancient feather pillow and some moth-eaten blankets lying discarded in the corner. Also – and this was where I prided myself on my detective skills – the creaking floorboards showed four indents where the legs of a heavy bed had once rested. The room was directly over the front door, and from the window I had a great view of the garden, or what was left of it.

There were three other rooms on the first floor, and all were empty, but the stairs up to the next landing were almost completely missing, only the banisters remained intact, so I decided that it wouldn't be wise to try climbing up: a fall of one storey was bad enough, but two storeys might be fatal. Looking back, I think that was probably the only wise decision I'd made that day.

Downstairs, at the back of the house, was a huge old kitchen. The walls were damp and covered with large patches of fungus. An ancient cracked sink was against the wall, though it had clearly been a long time since it had contained water; long blades of grass were growing up through the plug hole.

And, aside from odd items of broken furniture, that was all there was. But it was enough to keep me exploring for far too long. It was only when I noticed that it was too dark to see my watch that I realised how late it was. Within seconds, it seemed, the sky clouded over, and it started to rain. I stood for a long time in the shelter of the doorway, waiting out the rain. As the evening grew darker, I began to feel more and more stupid. What was I doing there? How could I have left my rucksack behind? How was I going to find my way back in the dark?

After a long time, the pounding rain finally stopped, but by then it was almost completely dark, and I decided that I'd be safer waiting in the house until morning. Another bad decision.

I managed to get a small fire going, but it wasn't really enough to keep out the bitter cold. I was only wearing a light jacket, and I toyed with the idea of taking the jacket off for a few minutes, then putting it back on again, so I'd feel warmer, but I knew that it wouldn't really help.

The floor was cold, and my backside grew numb, so I had to keep getting up and stretching every half an hour or so.

It was the fourth or fifth time I got up – I can't remember exactly which – when I heard the noise. I stopped in mid-stretch, and listened, but all I could hear was the pounding of my heart.

I took a deep breath, and called out, "Hello?"
Silence.
"Is there anyone here?" I called.

My own voice echoed slightly through the house, and that made the silence seem even worse.

Then I heard it again, and this time I was able to tell what the sound was. It was a young boy or a young girl, crying softly. I suddenly realised that I probably wasn't the only one sheltering in the house. Perhaps someone else had got lost in the woods . . . a child separated from their parents. Or, a darker side of myself suggested, it could be an escaped lunatic. Or worse. But by that stage, I didn't care. I was cold, tired and hungry. At least an escaped lunatic would be someone to talk to.

So I checked that the fire was OK, and began to wander around the ground floor of the house. It was completely dark, the only light came from my small fire, and as I left the room I found myself engulfed in the darkness, as though I was swallowed up by the night.

"This is useless," I whispered to myself. "I can't see a thing!"

But I walked on anyway, keeping my fingertips against the walls as a guide. The room I'd been in was at the front of the house – it looked as though it had once been a parlour or something – and I was moving towards the rear. I tried to picture the layout of the house as I remembered it from earlier during the day, but it wasn't easy. I was walking in total darkness, and must have been taking small steps, because the house seemed much larger than before. Occasionally my feet kicked against some piece of debris, and I had to reach out with my foot to see if it was something I could go around or climb over.

My imagination wasn't helping. Every time I passed a doorway I could imagine something reaching out to grab me, to lock its bony hands around my neck, to drag me screaming and crying into its lair . . . Or I'd reach out with my foot and feel something soft, feel it move slightly under my foot, then it would scurry away briefly, its many legs skittering across the hard floor, to stop and turn, and stare at me with angry red eyes . . .

I almost screamed when I walked straight into a wall. I'd bashed my nose and forehead, and for a few seconds I staggered around in a little circle, clutching my nose and calling myself all sorts of names for being so stupid.

When I recovered, I suddenly realised that I'd completely lost my bearings. I put my hands out in front of me, and walked slowly forward, trying to reach a wall. Then it happened again: something hit me in the face even though my hands were outstretched.

This time I *did* scream. I lashed out blindly with my fists, hoping to hit whatever was in front of me.

And then I realised that I'd walked into the side of the staircase in the hall, and that I'd been walking under the stairs. I giggled to myself, relieved that there was nothing more dangerous than a few planks of wood in my way. I told myself that the most dangerous thing in the house was probably me.

Now that I knew exactly where I was, I decided to return to the fire. There hadn't been anyone crying, it was just my imagination. Or maybe it was a cat outside, or something like that. And then I heard it again: a child's voice, there was no doubt. It was sobbing softly.

I froze. I could feel the hairs on my arms standing up, and my mouth was suddenly dry. Worse than that, my hands were beginning to shake.

"Who's there?" I called, trying to keep my voice steady. "Is there anyone here?"

The sobbing stopped, and from somewhere above I thought I could hear footsteps. Slow, dragging footsteps, scraping across the wooden floorboards.

Then a voice, trembling and sorrowful, "Help me."

I almost ran from the house there and then. I wanted

to burst through the front door and keep going, out into the woods. I didn't care what might be out there, I didn't care that I might get lost, or that I might fall into a ditch and drown. All I wanted to do was get away.

But I couldn't. I knew that if there was a child trapped in the house, I'd never forgive myself if I didn't try to help. So I took a deep breath, and called "Hold on! I'm coming! Which room are you in?"

There was no answer, not even the sobbing.

Reaching out carefully, I grabbed hold of the banisters and began to climb the stairs. I remembered from earlier during the day that several of the stairs were missing or very weak, so I had to move forward slowly. If I slipped or fell . . .

As I climbed, I called out again, "You have to tell me where you are! Hello? How can I find you if you won't tell me?"

I was sweating when I finally reached the top. I clung on to the banister post and tried to catch my breath. After a few minutes, I felt able to continue searching.

"Hello? Where are you?"

The voice drifted back to me. "Help me. I'm scared. They left me behind."

"Who did?" I asked. "Who left you?"

There was a pause, then the voice said, "Everybody. They never came back for me."

"What's your name?"

"Peter."

I listened carefully, trying to locate the source of the voice, but there were too many echoes. "You have to tell me where you are!" I said. "I can't find you!" There was silence again. I sighed. Finding this poor kid wasn't going to be easy. He was probably scared out of his wits. "OK," I called. "You just keep talking, all right? I'll follow the sound of your voice."

Again, there was no answer.

"Why don't you sing a song?" I suggested, trying to sound more cheerful than I felt. "Sing me your favourite song, Peter."

Then, very faintly, I heard him begin to sing. His voice was clear, but weak. "Ring a ring a rosie, pocket full of posies, atishoo, atishoo, we all fall down."

I tilted my head left and right as he sang. "Again, Peter. That was very good."

This time I was able to tell where the sound was coming from: the second floor. I swallowed. I hadn't tried to get up there in daylight, it was far too dangerous, but now, in complete darkness, it would be madness.

"Peter! You'll have to come out on to the landing! The stairs are gone, and I can't get up to you!" As soon as I said it, I realised that it was a stupid thing to say. Of course Peter knew that the stairs were gone. How could he not know?

Then I began to wonder how he managed to get up there himself. "Peter, is there another way up? Is there another set of stairs?"

He began to cry again.

"All right!" I called. "I'll give it a go, OK? Keep singing for me, Peter."

I tried to picture the banisters up to the second floor. The stairs had mostly rotted away, but the banisters had looked strong. I convinced myself that they'd be able to take my weight. I climbed carefully on to the thick

31

banister, lying flat against it with my arms and legs looped around it, then I began to pull myself up. It was the hardest thing I've ever done. I inched my way up to the top, praying that the banisters wouldn't collapse under me, hoping that the floorboards would be intact when I reached the top. My hands were slippery with sweat, and several times I had to stop and carefully wipe them on the backside of my jeans.

Peter was singing continuously, the same song over and over, and by that stage I wanted to get to the top just so that I could get him to shut up.

But I made it, and eventually stood panting and sweating on the second storey landing. "All right, Peter," I gasped. "I'm here. Which room are you in?"

Again, there was silence.

As I moved carefully along the landing, I became aware of the smell. It was like a mixture of perfume and rotting meat, as though someone had tried to mask a foul smell.

And then I noticed a faint light flickering from the room ahead of me. "Peter? Are you in there?"

His voice, when it came, was very weak. "I'm here."

I reached out and pushed open the door. It was a bedroom, in much better condition than the rest of the house. It was lit by two small oil lamps, and all around the walls were vases of fresh flowers. In the centre of the room, dwarfed by the huge bed, was a young boy.

I smiled. "Peter?"

He nodded, tears of relief in his eyes. "I didn't think anyone would ever come for me."

I sat on the edge of the bed and looked at him carefully. He couldn't have been more than five years old, though he had none of the plumpness you'd expect from someone of that age. His arms and neck were incredibly thin, and his eyes were dark-rimmed, having sunk back into their sockets. He raised a hand feebly towards me, and I took it. He was cold.

But his skin was the most alarming thing. It was almost transparent, the purple veins showing clearly, and it was marked with red circular sores. I lifted his arm high – he winced slightly in pain – and I could see large swellings in his armpits, like huge boils.

I lowered his arm slowly, and swallowed. "Peter, what happened?"

"They left me," he said, turning his eyes towards me. "They went away."

"Who did? Who was it? Your family?"

He nodded. "Momma and Poppa."

It was then that I noticed where the bad smell was coming from; it was from Peter himself. Suddenly I was disgusted. Not because the boy was sick, but because he had been abandoned, left to die.

"Peter, how long have you been here?"

He shrugged. "I don't know. A long time."

"What's wrong with you? What are these sores?"

He smiled slightly. "Ring a ring a rosie."

I didn't understand – not then, not for a long time – but I put on a brave face. "In the morning we'll get out of here, OK? We'll bring you to a hospital, and then we'll try to find your family."

He gripped my hand with sudden strength. "Thank you. No one else ever came back for me. But you did."

I patted his hand.

"Will you stay here with me? Until the morning?

None of the others would wait, you see. They didn't want to see me die."

"Peter, you're not going to die, all right? I'll get you to a hospital in the morning." Though even as I comforted him, I was wondering exactly *how* I'd get him out of the house. Just getting past the stairs would be difficult enough.

I found an old blanket, and lay down across the end of the bed. I didn't think I'd be able to sleep, but suddenly it was morning. The sun was streaming through the uncurtained window, and dazzled me when I opened my eyes. I sat up and stretched, and turned to see if Peter was awake yet.

The bed was empty. I looked around the room. Two broken vases were the only remains of the hundreds of fresh flowers. The oil lamps were broken and rusted, and the bed was battered and worn.

I searched the room thoroughly, but there was no doubt; no one had lived in that room for hundreds of years. I fled from the room, half-slid down the banisters, and out of the house. I never went back.

It took me a long time, but piece by piece, I put it all together. In the middle of the seventeenth century, Europe was riddled by the Black Death, the bubonic plague. It wasn't very virulent in Ireland, but someone in Peter's family must have unwittingly brought it from England, maybe his father, whom I later learned was a travelling businessman.

And when his family discovered that their son was infected, they couldn't stand to watch him die. They filled his room with flowers to cover the smell, then left him, abandoned him.

All the time the boy hung on, waiting for someone to come back to him, and he was too young to fully understand what had happened. The only thing he had were the words of a song:

"Ring a ring a rosie,
Pocket full of posies,
Atishoo, atishoo,
We all fall down."

# THE CORPSE WILL WALK

*Carolyn Swift*

The rain spattered against the carriage window as the train pulled out of Heuston Station, but it made no difference to Nora. The engineering works at Inchicore would have been blurred in any case. When her mother had offered her the window seat so she would be able to see the new lambs in the fields as they passed she had been glad, but not because of the lambs. It gave her an excuse to keep her head turned away from the others.

"He was 84," her mother had said, "and no one lives for ever. He'd had a good life and died peacefully in his sleep. Sure, wasn't it a grand way to go? He'd have hated to be tied to his bed and a burden on us all, so there's no call to be crying. Look at me! He was my father and I'm not crying."

All Nora could think of was that this time when they got to Athenry there would be no Granda to meet them, his blue eyes twinkling and the white hair around the back of his head fluffed up like a robin's feathers on

36

a wet day. He may have been her mother's Dadda, Nora thought, but he got on much better with her. She thought of how the two of them would be off in a twinkling across the fields in search of mushrooms or fraughan as her mother called after him, "Really, Dad, you're worse than she is!"

There would be no more stories now about the strange things that had happened to him or to 'a woman I know' or to 'a man from a neighbouring parish'. Some of the stories were scary, too, about the banshee that wailed amongst the trees whenever one of the Glynns died, or the foxes that gathered around the castle the time the old lord lay on his death bed. Still, sitting around the fire with the smell of the turf smoke twitching her nostrils, it was a nice sort of scary and Nora had never ever thought of Granda himself dying.

As the train stopped with a jerk at Portarlington Station, the smoke from her father's pipe drifted across the carriage in the draught from the open door and made her cough. Immediately she could hear her grandfather's voice, almost as if he were sitting by her side.

"Carry on with the coughin', Nora," he chuckled, as he always did. "The corpse'll walk!"

The first time he had said it, she hadn't understood what he meant.

"Don't mind him," her mother had told her, seeing the puzzled look on her face. "He must have his little joke. It's a pun on the word 'coughing'. Carry on with the coffin, the corpse will walk."

Funny, Nora thought now, how so many of Granda's jokes were to do with death, only now it wasn't funny at all.

"May I have your attention, please! We will shortly be arriving at Athenry Station. Next stop Athenry."

At the familiar words coming over the train's sound system, Nora could no longer hold back the tears. How excited she had always felt when she heard those words, wondering what surprise her grandfather had for her this time. There might be three little furry kittens hidden away in the straw in the corner of the barn, or maybe a new little calf for her to visit on the farm at the end of the lane. But this time there would be no Granda with a finger to his lips, pulling her aside to whisper some secret for her ears alone. Clutching her case, she followed her mother down from the train and out of the station to the big black car that was waiting to drive them to Granda's house.

It looked strange with the curtains drawn in the daytime and, even though Aunt Tina came to the gate to meet them, it seemed oddly silent without the sound of Granda's stick, tapping merrily along the flagged path, and his mischievous chuckle as he winked at her to let her know he had something to tell her as soon as her parents were out of the way.

"Come and say good-bye to your Granda," Aunt Tina said, taking her by the hand and leading her into the parlour.

But inside the long wooden box on the parlour table there was only a grey-faced old man with his eyes closed.

"That's not Granda!" Nora cried.

"Don't be silly," her mother snapped, but Aunt Tina took her in her arms and kissed her saying, "True, for your Granda's in heaven now. It's only his corpse that's there."

Dressed in her best clothes, Nora sat beside Aunt Tina in the car, driving slowly along the road to the church behind the big, black hearse which held the long wooden box, its lid now firmly nailed down.

"Where's Dadda going?" Nora asked, as her father, looking strange in his black tie, left them to join Uncle Matt and his two sons beside the hearse.

"He's going to carry in the coffin," Aunt Tina explained, and again Nora seemed to hear her grandfather chuckle: "Carry on with the coughin', the corpse'll walk!"

But though her father carried one corner of the coffin on his shoulder and Uncle Matt and cousins Tom and Pat carried the other three corners, no corpse got out of it and walked, though Nora kept her eyes on it all through the prayers and afterwards, while the people were filing past them, saying how they were sorry for their trouble.

That night Nora tossed and turned in the bed in the little room next to the one that had been her grandfather's. It seemed to her that someone kept tapping on the window, though Aunt Tina said it was only the branches of the old oak tree, blown by the wind that was rising from the west. Only when Aunt Tina put a small night-light on the little table beside her bed, so Nora could see that nothing lurked in the shadows behind the wardrobe, did she finally fall asleep.

She was awakened by a strange rumbling sound and the noise of horses' hoofbeats. It was still dark in her room, apart from the tiny pool of faint light around her night-light, but a silvery finger of moonlight poked through the slit between the drawn curtains towards her bed. The hoofbeats seemed to stop right outside her window, as she heard the neighing of the horses, and Nora thought there must be travellers' ponies loose on the road. Shivering a little, she slid out of bed and went across to the window, pulling aside the right-hand curtain. Then she screamed, a scream so long and piercing that Aunt Tina came running into the room, the grey hair she normally wore in a bun loose around her shoulders. When she saw Nora's white face and staring eyes, the pupils big and dark with fear and her mouth still wide from screaming, she pulled her away from the window and on to her bed, wrapping the old-fashioned quilt around her for warmth.

"What's wrong, pet?" she cried. "Hush, now, or your poor mother will think you're being murdered in your bed."

"The *coiste-bodhar*!" Nora sobbed. "It's outside the gate now."

"You only dreamed it, pet," Aunt Tina soothed. "I should never have taken you to see your Granda, only the two of you were always such pals I thought you'd want to see the last of him. But 'twas too much of a shock for you and it's given you nightmares."

"No!" Nora cried, "I did see it! It was just the way Granda described it. Right outside in the moonlight: a big old coach like the one in the shed at Moylans, with two black horses and a coachman up in front, but the coachman had no head!"

Aunt Tina walked over to the window and drew back the curtains so that bright moonlight flooded the room.

"There's nothing there, pet, I promise you," she said.

"Come and see for yourself."

But Nora only pulled the quilt over her head. When Aunt Tina tried to draw her over to the window, she struggled with her, clinging to the bed.

"Maybe *you* can't see it," she sobbed, "but it's there. And an old man with a thin, white, bony face, wearing a long black shroud got out of it and looked straight at me before he turned and sort of glided away."

"It was a nightmare, pet," Aunt Tina repeated, "look!"

And with surprising strength for her mother's elder sister, whom Nora had always thought frail, she forced the struggling, sobbing girl to the window. Nora closed her eyes tight shut, afraid to look. After a while, however, hearing nothing but her aunt's pleas to her to look, she opened her eyes a small chink. The branches of the old oak tree stirred in the strengthening wind but, where only moments ago the coach had stood in the moonlight, now there was nothing but an old cardboard box, blown from heaven knows where.

"You see, pet," her aunt said gently. "There's nothing there."

"But I heard the rumbling of the wheels," Nora insisted. "That's what woke me."

"It was probably thunder," Aunt Tina told her. "There's a storm forecast. I thought we'd have had it here before this. Now, be a good girl and get back into bed and I'll bring you up a mug of warm milk that will help you sleep. Heaven only knows we all need a good night's rest before facing into the funeral in the morning."

"I'd be scared to close my eyes for fear the *coiste-bodhar* would come back," Nora said but in the end she did, never opening them again until her mother shook her.

"Hurry, Nora," she said, "and get yourself washed and dressed. We've all too much to do this morning to be up and down the stairs calling you."

The sky was dark and threatening, but the storm Aunt Tina had talked about had still not arrived. Ashamed of having woken her aunt, Nora leaped out of bed, hoping her father and mother knew nothing of what had happened. In this, however, she was disappointed.

"I hope you apologised to Aunt Tina for disturbing her night's sleep," her mother said to her over breakfast. "As if she hadn't troubles enough just now."

"Sure, she couldn't help it," her aunt cut in, before Nora could say anything. "She cried out in her sleep. It's no great wonder for she's as upset as the rest of us."

"Would you believe I never heard a thing?" her father exclaimed, "but then I supposed I'd be sleeping soundly after the day that was in it."

"You mean, after all the whiskey you put away," her mother corrected him, but her father only said, "Wouldn't the neighbours think badly of me if I hadn't taken a drink or two with them, the way your father would have done?"

The funeral was much like the removal the day before only much, much longer and this time Nora sat dry-eyed, only crying afterwards in the graveyard when they lowered the coffin into the big hole they had opened up against the headstone with her grandmother's name on it. Then they laid a board over the hole, put her little bunch of early primroses on top of it amongst all the wreaths and cut flowers and it was all over. And not a minute too soon either, Nora thought, as the rain that had been threatening all morning started to come down in sheets.

That evening, as they stood on the dimly-lit station platform with the blackness of the night all around them, waiting for the train from Galway, she felt her eyelids drooping. Again the neighbours had come back to the house and she had helped her mother and Aunt Tina to hand round plates of sandwiches and cups of tea, while her father looked after the drinks. Now, as she sat on the little bench, her legs swinging, her eyes began to close.

Suddenly a rumble of thunder jerked her awake. For a moment she was panic-stricken, thinking it was the rumble of the *coiste-bodhar* returning, until she saw where she was. Then she heard the rumble of the approaching train, as the 6:25 from Galway pulled into the station. The engine went past her up the platform in a whiff of diesel oil, making her cough and once again she thought of her grandfather and his little joke.

"Come along," her mother said impatiently, making for the door of the carriage right in front of them.

Just as they got to it the door opened and out of it stepped an old man with a thin, white, bony face. He was wearing a long, shapeless black cape and for a moment he looked straight at Nora, before turning and moving off down the platform towards the exit with a strange, gliding walk. With a scream, Nora turned and ran in the opposite direction. Her father hurried after her and caught her by the arm.

"What's wrong with you?" he demanded. "Have you gone crazy?"

"I'm not getting on that train!" Nora cried.

"Don't be ridiculous," her father said. "How am I to get to work in the morning?"

As her mother caught up with them, the guard began slamming the carriage doors shut.

"Hurry up or we'll miss the train!" she shouted.

With that her husband snatched up the struggling Nora in his arms and carried her bodily on to the train, throwing her down into the window seat of the nearest carriage as the guard blew his whistle and the train started to move off.

"Now," her father said as the train gathered speed, "perhaps you'll be good enough to tell us what all that nonsense was about?"

"It was like my dream!" Nora sobbed.

"I never heard such rubbish!" her father snapped, but her mother put a hand on his arm.

"How d'you mean, like your dream?" she asked, but Nora seemed unable to explain.

"As if the funeral wasn't bad enough," her father began, but again his wife cut in.

"Try to be patient with her," she said. "It's that has her so upset."

It was at that moment that they all heard a sudden terrible bellowing and a screeching of brakes. The whole train seemed to shake and Nora found herself flung across the carriage. There was an awful crashing sound, her mother screamed and all the lights in the carriage went out as the train shuddered to a stop.

From the darkness outside, Nora heard a strange

confusion of screams, cries and hurried footsteps. Stumbling to her feet, she peered out of the window, but only a faint flickering light like that of a hand-held torch beam could be seen through the rain-streaked glass. Suddenly there was a flash of lightning and, for a brief second, she saw the tail end of the train on the curve of the track, the last carriages tipped over on their sides like a line of coffins. Then all was darkness and confusion once more, until the sound of approaching sirens drowned the other noises. Someone wrenched open the carriage door.

"Is everyone all right in there?" came a man's voice out of the darkness.

"Yes, thank God!" her mother replied. "What happened?"

"Cattle on the line at Ballyboggen crossing," the man said. "The storm must have scared them into stampeding in front of the engine. The last five carriages are derailed and we've instructions to get all passengers out."

"It's lashing rain," her mother protested, reluctant to leave the shelter of the carriage for the storm raging outside.

"They're bringing up buses," the man said. "Come on, I'll help you down."

It was a long drop to the tracks, but Nora's father lifted her down into the arms of the man standing below, who lowered her gently on to the grass beside the track. Struggling with their cases towards the line of waiting buses through the long wet grass, rain slanting into their faces and thunder still rumbling overhead, Nora heard again the bellowing of the injured bullocks.

It was like her nightmare all over again, only with thunder in place of the rumbling of the coach wheels and the cries of the cattle instead of the neighing of the horses. Only when they sat shivering on one of the buses, waiting for the last of the uninjured passengers to board, were they able to look back at the scene of the accident, where firemen were trying to free the dead and injured from the twisted metal of the toppled carriages.

Her mother gave Nora an odd look. Then she turned to her father. "Do you realise we would have been in one of those end carriages if Nora hadn't run off?" she asked.

"True," her father agreed. "So maybe we should be thankful for her nonsense after all."

"It wasn't nonsense," Nora said. "I know it now. It was a warning. Granda always said the *coiste-bodhar* was a warning of death. I think now it was Granda that sent it to me, the way I'd run away and not be killed."

Her father only smiled but, the more Nora thought about it, the more she felt sure that it was indeed her grandfather that had let her see the likeness of a walking corpse coming from one of the end carriages, carriages that were now like tombs for so many who had travelled in them.

# THE LAUGHING HOUSE

### Morgan Llywelyn

A top a hill in County Wexford the Dawsons finally found the home of their dreams. It was a rather gaunt, high-gabled farmhouse overlooking fertile fields. The place had a homely atmosphere. And best of all, they could, just barely, afford it.

After years of living with Joan's family, they would finally have a place of their own. They could hardly believe their good fortune when the estate agent told them the price. Joan actually laughed aloud. "All our birthdays have come at once!" she exclaimed, staring with delight at the roses glowing in the flower bed beside the front door. She had always wanted roses.

Martin smiled at his plump, pretty wife. "The name of the house is perfect," he commented, pointing to the neat sign that hung on the gate-pillar. "'The Laughing House'. And we are people who like to laugh!"

Joan was in love with the place from the beginning. Even the stresses of moving day could not spoil her good humour. Her mood communicated itself to the three small Dawson children, Colin, Mary and Anthony, who were soon whooping with delight as they ran up the stairs and slid back down the banister.

Martin Dawson frowned. "Don't be doing that now," he cautioned as he carried in a box of books. "You could hurt yourselves."

But his wife could not bear to spoil the little ones' fun. "There's nothing to hurt them," she pointed out. "The banister is broad and smooth, no splinters, and even if they take a tumble the stairs are thickly carpeted. Besides, when I was a girl I did the very same thing."

He gave in. He always gave in. He adored his family and could deny them nothing they wanted.

As she worked in her new kitchen, putting away dishes and saucepans, Joan could hear the children playing on the stairs. A glance out the window above the sink showed her Martin unloading still more boxes from their car at the side of the house. She began humming to herself, more content than she ever remembered being.

Then she heard the laugh.

It was a huge, bellowing, masculine laugh, that rumbled up as if from within some giant's belly and then burst full-throated into a great guffaw. Yet strangely, it was not happy laughter. Quite the opposite. The sound was brutal and cruel, like the very voice of evil.

A saucepan fell from Joan's startled fingers and clanged on the floor. "Jesus Mary and Joseph, who was that?" she cried.

She ran out into the hall just as Anthony, her youngest, lost his balance and fell off the banister. He let out a frightened howl, but when his mother swooped to pick him up he had no more than a bruised knee. He was badly frightened, however, and clung to his mother for a long time, whimpering softly. Mary and Colin stayed close also, casting occasional fearful glances into the shadows of the stairwell.

As she comforted her son, Joan almost forgot about the strange laugh. She only remembered it to tell Martin after he brought in the last of the boxes from the car.

"Are you certain it was a man's voice you heard?" he asked, frowning. "Here? In our house?"

"I told you, it wasn't a voice exactly. It was just a laugh. But it belonged to a man, all right, I know that much. And it was in the house, out in the hall where the children were playing."

"Did you hear it?" Martin asked his elder son, Colin.

The boy shook his tousled blond head. "I don't think so," he said cautiously. He did not want to remember the laugh. Just thinking about it gave him a sick feeling in his stomach.

"Well, I heard it," Joan insisted. "I want you to search the house, Martin, and find whoever it was."

Her husband sighed, but did as she asked. As he had expected, there was no one lurking in the house. No one at all. It was empty except for their own things and the smell of fresh paint and wallpaper. The house seemed as bright and cheerful as summer sunshine.

"You must have imagined that laughter," Martin told his wife. "We're all tired, sometimes the mind plays tricks."

Joan's eyes flashed with a rare anger. "I don't imagine

things, Martin Dawson! I know what I heard."

But in the busy days that followed, the incident faded from memory. Joan was almost convinced she had been imagining things – until late one afternoon when she heard the laughter again. It was the same voice: Male, unpleasant, humourless. But the laugh was not as loud as before.

This time Joan was in the bedroom, just crossing to the adjoining bathroom to get a glass of water from the tap. When the laughter suddenly rippled behind her she froze in her tracks, but when she turned around, no one was there.

A shudder ran across her shoulders.

She went on into the bathroom and took a bottle of aspirin from the shelf, then turned on the cold-water tap and held the drinking glass under it. But her hand was shaking. The glass slipped, fell into the porcelain sink and shattered. Somehow, one large shard flew upwards and sliced across Joan's exposed wrist, cutting deeply.

Blood spurted.

She cried aloud in shock.

When Martin came home from work that night, his wife showed him her bandaged wrist. "The doctor put in four stitches," she reported. Her voice sounded faint and her outstretched hand was trembling. The children, big-eyed, crowded around their mother.

"You say you dropped the glass when you heard that strange laugh again?" Martin asked.

"*Because* I heard that laugh again," Joan corrected.

"Are you blaming that for your accident?"

"I am." Her chin jutted forward stubbornly. "There

was something terribly wrong about that laughter. I know there was."

Martin turned to his oldest son. "Did you hear it, Colin?"

"I was outside," the boy claimed.

"Mary?" The little girl would not meet his eyes. "I was playing with my dolls," she said in a low voice.

"What about you, Anthony? Did you hear any strange laughter today – or when you fell off the banister?" The little lad shook his head. But Martin noticed that the child clung tightly to his mother's uninjured hand.

In his most reassuring voice, Martin told his family, "This is an old house, though it's new to us. Old houses creak and make noises. One of those noises must sound like a laugh, but there is no one really laughing, and you cannot blame accidents on groaning timbers. That's very silly." He grinned to show them how silly it was.

They smiled back at him, slowly.

They wanted to believe him. But in the days that followed they found themselves listening for the laugh. The children did not play as happily as they had done, and Joan grew increasingly nervous. The slightest thing made her start.

The fact that Martin did not seem to believe the laughter was really upsetting her. He had never doubted her before. Her normal good nature faded as the roses of summer were fading in the flowerbed. She and Martin began to argue, at first over little things, unimportant things. But the quarrels grew more frequent and more heated.

Lying in their beds at night, the children could hear

their parents' raised voices. They could hear something else, too; something that was very faint and far away in the beginning, but seemed to come closer as the days and nights passed.

They heard a voice laughing, somewhere in the house. A cold, cruel voice, taking pleasure from the arguments. The laughter the children heard was not loud, but muffled, as if whoever was making the sound was holding a hand over his mouth. But when Colin lay in the dark listening he found it very hard to imagine what sort of a hand was being held over what shape of mouth. The laughter was not human.

In the morning, as they ate their breakfast, Colin noticed that his sister Mary kept spilling her food. When he tried to catch her eye she would not look at him. When he asked her if she had heard the laughter, she would not answer him.

But he knew. Yet he did not speak of it. None of the children spoke of it, as if they feared that talking about the laughter would make it more real.

But it was real enough. Day by day, little Anthony was growing quieter and paler. Mary began to have nightmares. Colin, trying to be brave because he was the oldest, roamed the house, peering into cupboards, trying to find whoever was laughing. But he only did it in the daytime, and only when at least one of his parents was within calling distance.

Somewhere in the heart of the house something chuckled to itself, delighted with the growing smell of fear and anger that was replacing the freshness of paint and wallpaper.

Joan was never without an anguished awareness of

the laugh. She thought no one else heard it because the children never mentioned it. The sound, and her fear of the sound, haunted her days and nights. She longed to speak of it to Martin and have him comfort her and call her silly, but she could not do that any more. They were short-tempered with one another. He left for work early and began coming home later and later, avoiding the atmosphere in the house . . . the nervous, brittle wife, the increasingly silent children.

Only when he was away did the accidents occur. In time Joan realised that the type of laugh she heard was a peculiar form of warning. A roaring belly-laugh preceded a minor scrape or bruise, but the softer the laughter, the worse the trouble to come.

A whispery snigger warned Joan just before Martin crashed the car when he stormed out of the house after one of their worst arguments. The laugh had drifted through the hallways of the house like windblown sand. The children had heard it too, though they did not speak of it to their mother or each other. Their eyes were large and staring in their pale faces.

Martin Dawson spent weeks in the hospital in traction. During that time, his family never heard the laugh. Joan became convinced that it was something her husband had been doing somehow, to drive her mad. The children connected their father's absence with the absence of the laugh and began to believe he had been torturing them with the sound for reasons they could not imagine. They all dreaded the day Martin Dawson would come home again.

When at last he was released from the hospital, his wife went to collect him. She was tense, pale. He tried to put his arms around her but she pulled away, and on the journey home she hardly spoke to him.

The roses, he noted, had faded and died in the flower-bed, and the house looked bleak wreathed in autumn mist. It seemed very cold inside, although the fires were lit and the electric radiators were turned on.

The family Martin came home to were not the cheerful, happy people he had brought to "The Laughing House" months ago.

They all seemed to be waiting for something. Listening.

In desperation, at last Martin went to see a psychologist in Dublin, an old friend from his schooldays.

"You were under stress for a number of years, living with your wife's family," James Garrity told him. "Probably both Joan and the children felt that stress. Perhaps it is just coming to the surface now."

"But why does my wife insist she hears some evil laughter in the house? I've never heard it. Is she losing her mind?"

"Of course not," Garrity tried to reassure him. "There is a simple explanation. You say the name of your new house is 'The Laughing House'?"

Martin nodded. "It is."

"Well, there you have it. The name has worked on Joan's subconscious, it's the source of her ah, ghost, if you will. I could talk to her, if you like. How about the children, are they all right?"

"They are very quiet," Martin admitted. "But it is probably because their mother is acting strangely."

James Garrity nodded. "Bring her to see me, we'll put

this matter to rights before it gets any more serious."

But when Martin relayed the details of the conversation to Joan she lost her fragile temper. "You think there's something wrong with my mind," she shrieked. "You think I'm insane!"

"I do not!" Martin protested. "I only want to help you."

But she would not listen. She could not listen. At the back of her head, overriding Martin's words, a soft chuckle began and continued until it drowned out everything else. A soft, evil, mirthless chuckle that grew and grew until it filled Joan's throat and she began, helplessly, to laugh with it. To laugh and laugh, her lips curving but her eyes wild with fright, while Martin stared at her horrified.

They were in the kitchen. The children were playing outside. Although a cold and rainy autumn had set in they stayed out of the house as long as they could, only returning for meals or when the fall of night drove them indoors. They never spoke to each other of the reason. They did not discuss the laughter. It was simply there, an awful presence in the house. Talking about it would only bring it closer.

As they played outside that grey afternoon, they heard raised voices coming from inside the house. Then the sound of Joan's laughter, rising out of control. Colin stopped even pretending to play as a cold chill ran down his spine.

"Listen to Mam!" he gasped.

Mary and Anthony stopped to listen too. Tears welled up in Mary's blue eyes. Suddenly Anthony clapped his hands over his ears as if he could shut out the sound, but he could not.

It was in all their heads now, the sound of laughter. Sick laughter, mad laughter.

As the evil spirit gripped her, Joan tried to run from the kitchen as if she could somehow escape. But Martin did not understand, he thought she was trying to run away from him. He caught her by one arm and tried to hold on to her.

And all the time the laughter went on, low, nasty, vicious. Evil laughter. Taking control of Joan, twisting her thoughts . . . She was unaware when her hand reached for the bread knife on the kitchen counter.

Afterwards, the police took her away. Martin had to go back to hospital to have the deep stab wound in his shoulder treated. Joan's parents came for the children, who were badly shocked. "You will come home with us," they said, "until everything is sorted out." They did not add that it might take a very long time.

As Joan's mother looked around the house, her eyes taking in the many loving touches the Dawsons had introduced to make it home, she shook her head in disbelief. "I just don't understand this," she told her husband. "Martin says he wants to sell the house immediately. How can they give up such a perfect place?"

To her astonishment, young Colin began to laugh. It was not a child's laugh; it was cold and mirthless and gave his grandmother a sick feeling in the pit of her stomach. Then Mary joined in, her soft little-girl's voice stained with something ugly. Anthony began to chuckle in a way no small boy should ever chuckle, as if he knew some dark and terrible secret that was giving him great pleasure.

Three small children standing huddled together in what had been their home, laughing unnatural laughter on the most tragic day of their young lives. The sound seemed to resonate in the walls and floorboards, as if the entire house was laughing with them. Their alarmed grandparents hurried them away.

Now the former Dawson house stands empty on its hilltop. When summer comes again the roses will bloom in the flower-bed beside the front door. A "For Sale" sign hangs just below the sign that proudly announces the name of the high-gabled timber farmhouse. "The Laughing House", reads the sign. And though no one is there to hear, a low gurgle of laughter constantly ripples through the rooms.

# A RATTLY-CHAINS AND HOWLY GHOST

*Jane Mitchell*

Last Monday, Patrick Vaughan brought a ghost in for the Nature Table in our classroom. Before the weekend, teacher had said that the *Cigire* was coming to visit our school on Monday to test all the pupils and visit the classrooms. He was definitely coming to our class because it's right next-door to the Headmistress's office. The best class in the school is always the one right next door to the office and the *Cigire* is certain to visit the best class in the school. It's the one he really wants to see. Because that's our class this year, he'd be sure to come in, teacher said.

When teacher told us on Friday about the *Cigire* coming, we all gasped in shock. We weren't that shocked really, but we knew there was some kind of shocking news coming and we were ready. The Headmistress had been in to whisper to our teacher and our teacher gasped in shock and looked round the walls. So when she told us, we gasped in shock and looked round the walls too.

Our walls are covered in our paintings and stories and projects. It's always good to have the walls covered like that for the *Cigire*. We had our projects about hyacinth bulbs and daffodils above the Nature Table. We had our Irish essays about the birds building their nests and hatching their eggs pinned up beside the door. The wall behind the library was covered with our reviews on 'Books about Spring' and above the sink, we had a big wall frieze tracing the routes taken by migratory birds returning to Ireland in the springtime. The classroom looked really well. Except for one thing. It wasn't spring. It was autumn. And nearly Hallowe'en too. That was why we all gasped and looked round. The *Cigire* likes to see paintings and projects and stories, but he doesn't like to see them when they're six months out of date. And especially not in the best class in the school. There's no knowing what everyone else has in *their* classrooms.

Luckily for us, the *Cigire* was decent enough to phone on Friday morning to tell us he was coming on Monday. Otherwise he would have caught us celebrating spring in the autumn. *We* all knew it wasn't springtime, and that we had been too busy to change the walls, but he wasn't to know that. What would he have thought?

After we got over the shock, teacher wrote a long list of all the things that we'd have to change in the classroom before Monday. Then she divided the jobs out among us. After little break, we had to heap our schoolbags in the library corner and roll up our sleeves. We tore down all the paintings and projects and stories. We put them into big black plastic bags that the

Headmistress ran in and gave us. The Headmistress was running into all the classrooms and giving them black plastic bags.

Angela O'Connor began to cry when her poem about the woods in springtime was thrown out. It was her best poem ever and teacher had given her a gold star for it. Teacher said to Angela that if she didn't stop crying, she'd be *seeing* gold stars and no doubt about it. Angela stopped crying.

Alan and Sam, the twins, had to clear the Nature Table. Alan threw out all the springtime twigs, but teacher said to put them back again because the buds had dried up and gone black, so now they looked like autumn twigs. Sam asked teacher what he should do with the black jelly in the plastic box on the Nature Table. Teacher was standing on a chair balanced on my desk at the time. She was trying to take the Christmas mobile off the ceiling and she didn't answer at first. So while he was waiting, Sam sat down with the box of black jelly so we could all have a look. It wobbled in the plastic box and had green furry stuff over the top of it. Sam shook the box to make it wobble more and this horrible smell came out. Joseph O'Brien stuck his ruler into it and balanced a blob of the jelly on the end of it. He tried to chase Eileen Murray with it, but it fell off his ruler and landed with a plop on the floor.

Teacher was finished taking the mobile down by then. She was very cross with Joseph and made him clean up the jelly and apologise to Eileen. Then, she had a look at the box of black jelly. At first, teacher didn't know what it was either. Then she remembered. The black jelly was tadpoles and frog spawn from

Elizabeth Burke's father's pond. Elizabeth brought them in last spring and we did projects about the life-cycle of the tadpole. Our life-cycle didn't include that they turned to black jelly after being tadpoles. Sam was sent to flush the smelly jelly down the boys' toilet.

By big lunch, the classroom looked very bare. The Headmistress sent a huge rubbish-bin on wheels round all the classrooms to gather up the black plastic bags. We ate our lunches and looked at the bare walls. The only thing left on them were some blobs of blue-tac and the streak of jam above the blackboard from Ian's jam sandwich last Easter.

While we were eating, teacher wrote down another list of what had to be done in the afternoon.

After big lunch, we worked in our groups. The Apple group had to make a crepe-paper collage of a pumpkin. The Orange group drew pictures of what animals go into hibernation in the Autumn. The Bananas wrote Irish stories about Hallowe'en, and the Peaches went to the big school library to find out about Hallowe'en celebrations in other countries. The Grapes were sent out to the yard to look for things for the Nature Table.

By half-past two, we had lots of Autumn pictures and stories to pin up on the walls. The classroom looked really well and teacher was very happy. She was so happy that she let us off homework for the weekend. She sat at her desk and looked round the classroom. Then she frowned.

The only thing that didn't look too well was the Nature Table. The Grapes hadn't been able to find anything in the yard, and all that was on the Nature

Table were the twigs left over from spring. Then Patrick Vaughan put up his hand.

"Teacher," he said. "I can bring something in for the Nature Table."

Teacher was a little unsure. The last person to say that was Joseph O'Brien and he had brought in a cockroach in a matchbox. It got out and terrorised the class – until teacher got really angry and terrorised the class instead, so we all sat down again. Joseph O'Brien spent the rest of the day in the Headmistress's office. The cockroach escaped. But it wasn't Joseph O'Brien this time, it was Patrick Vaughan.

"What is it you have, Patrick?"

"Teacher, I found it on the beach last week."

"Has it to do with Autumn?"

"No, teacher, but it's to do with Hallowe'en. It's in a big glass jar."

Teacher smiled and swung on the back legs of her chair like she's always telling us not to.

"And what is it in the big glass jar that's to do with Hallowe'en, Patrick?"

"Teacher, it's a ghost."

Teacher burst out laughing and told us that because we'd worked so hard all day, she'd let us go home early.

She thought Patrick Vaughan was only joking. But he wasn't.

On Monday morning, we met Patrick in the yard before the bell rang.

"Where's your ghost?" we asked.

"Right here," said Patrick.

Under his arm he had a plastic bag. Inside the bag was a glass jar wrapped in a towel.

"There's no ghost in there," said Joseph O'Brien.

"There is so," argued Patrick.

"Let's hear him moaning then," challenged Joseph.

"OK," answered Patrick. He shook the jar really hard and we could hear groaning and moaning and chains rattling. Angela O'Connor screamed and ran away.

"What was it doing on the beach?" asked Eileen Murray.

"The tide washed it up," said Patrick.

"So how come you found it?" Sam enquired.

"I was walking the dog," replied Patrick.

"Where's it from?" Alan wanted to know.

"Made in Hong Kong," answered Patrick.

The bell rang then and we had to get in line to go to class. Teacher brought us in. She was wearing a new skirt for the *Cigire*.

After we had hung up our coats and had roll-call, Patrick put his hand up.

"Teacher, will I put the ghost on the Nature Table?"

Teacher wasn't in as happy a mood as she had been on Friday afternoon. She was fussed. She kept looking at her watch and checking the carpark for the *Cigire's* car.

"Oh, Patrick," she replied, "I've no time for your jokes this morning."

"But teacher . . . " began Patrick, standing up.

"No, no. I don't want to hear 'but teacher' this morning. Now sit down please."

Patrick looked worried, but he sat down in his seat. We all knew by teacher's voice that we had to be as quiet as mice or else there'd be skin and hair flying. But the ghost didn't know that. Beneath Patrick's chair, the glass jar, in its towel and plastic bag, rolled to and fro. We could hear a moaning sound. Teacher didn't hear the moaning sound. She began to hear our tables instead.

By the time we got to the five times tables, the ghost's moaning had turned into a howling noise. Patrick leaned under his chair and gave the jar a comforting little rock. The howling softened a bit, but Patrick looked very worried. As soon as he stopped rocking the jar, the howling got louder again.

By the end of the eight times tables, even teacher had noticed the noise.

"Hush," she said, raising her finger to her lips. "Hush and listen."

We all hushed, but we didn't have to listen. Nor did teacher, because the ghost's howling was so loud by then that we could all hear it quite clearly. Teacher looked at Joseph O'Brien right away.

"Joseph," her voice was very cross. "Joseph, what are you doing?" Joseph went red. He wasn't doing anything.

"I'm not doing anything," he told teacher.

"Then what is making that awful shrieking noise?"

Angela O'Connor was crying again – she was scared of the ghost. Teacher saw her.

"Angela O'Connor," she said, putting her hands on her hips, "if that noise is you crying because of your poem that got thrown out, I'll be *so* annoyed."

But Angela shook her head and teacher knew the noise wasn't coming from her. Patrick put his hand up.

"Teacher," he called.

"Yes, Patrick?"

"Teacher, it's the ghost," Patrick told her.

"Oh, for goodness sake, Patrick," teacher said, "if you don't stop carrying on with this silly joke, it'll be the Headmistress's office for you. Now who is making the noise?"

Teacher's voice was getting louder, because she was really angry and because she had to shout to be heard over the noise of the ghost who was shrieking and howling and rattling chains furiously now.

Just then, the door of the classroom opened and in walked the Headmistress. She was smiling very stiffly, and then we saw why. Behind her was the *Cigire*. He was smiling at us. We all stood up immediately and welcomed the two of them. When we stood up, Patrick knelt down very quickly and began to rock the jar and talk to the ghost. The noise got softer and nearly died away completely, but not quite. Teacher smiled too and they all stood and smiled at each other until the Headmistress turned and left. Then we sat down again.

The *Cigire* and teacher went over to the desk and began to talk quietly. While they talked, Patrick rocked the jar and talked to the ghost. We all turned in our seats to watch him, but this time, the ghost had had enough of the rocking and continued to moan out loud.

Teacher lifted her head from the books that she and the *Cigire* were looking at and gave Patrick a stony stare. The *Cigire* straightened up, cleared his throat and smiled. He too turned to Patrick.

"Well, young man," said the *Cigire*. "And what have we here?"

"It's a ghost," said Patrick.

"Is it indeed?" smiled the *Cigire*, giving our teacher a

65

sideways glance. He didn't believe Patrick either.

"And what sort of ghost is it?" asked the *Cigire*.

"It's a rattly-chains and howly ghost," answered Patrick.

The *Cigire* put his hands behind his back and strolled down to Patrick's desk. He stopped in front of it.

"Isn't that lovely. It's certainly rattling and howling this morning," shouted the *Cigire* above the noise of the ghost. "Why do you have a ghost in the classroom this morning?"

"Because teacher needed something about Autumn and Hallowe'en for the Nature Table," hollered Patrick, "so I said I'd bring my ghost in."

"So why isn't it on the Nature Table, teacher?" laughed the *Cigire*, turning to teacher.

Teacher went a pink colour. She smiled stiffly at the *Cigire*. She didn't really know what to say.

"Oh, now, *a Chigire!*" was all she said in the end.

The *Cigire* turned back to Patrick.

"Why is this ghost making so much noise?"

"Because it's scared of the dark," Patrick told him.

"But it's not dark in here," the *Cigire* pointed out, looking round the classroom.

"The ghost's in a jar in a towel in a plastic bag and it's dark under the wrappings," Patrick explained.

"Well, well, well," lamented the *Cigire*. "Why don't you let him out into the daylight for some fresh air?"

Patrick looked at the *Cigire*. Then he looked at teacher. Then slowly, he lifted the wrapped ghost up on the table. He took the jar and the towel out of the plastic bag. He unwrapped the towel from the jar. He stood the big glass jar on the table.

We all looked.

Inside the jar was the ghost. He was green and misty and he flickered, like a bright light, around the inside of the jar. He had glowing eyes and a long smoky tail. He stopped howling and, instead, looked round at everyone.

"Now, young man," said the *Cigire* crossly to Patrick after peering at the ghost. "What sort of computer game is this, then?"

Patrick looked at him, puzzled.

"It's a ghost," he said. As if to back him up, the ghost rattled some invisible chains and moaned a little. "It's a ghost for the Nature Table."

The *Cigire* was angry. He still didn't believe Patrick, even though he could see the ghost sitting in the jar on the table. He picked up the jar and shook it, hard.

"Stop," shouted Patrick. "You'll hurt him."

The ghost stopped howling, and gave a small whimper. The *Cigire* shook the jar again, and tried to prise open the lid. Patrick's eyes widened.

"No, no, you mustn't," he cried.

Inside the jar, the ghost snapped and growled at the *Cigire*. The lid was loosened and then the jar was open. There was a whizzing noise as the ghost zipped out and flickered all round our classroom. We could see the green, dazzling light zooming up to the ceiling and down to the floor. It flashed across the windows and shimmered past the door – howling and screeching all the time. We could hear teeth gnashing and chains rattling as the ghost bolted towards the *Cigire*. Then, in one sudden flash, the ghost – with a loud fizzle – darted down the neck of the *Cigire's* shirt. The *Cigire* leaped up in the air with fright. He gave a great shiver, and at the same time, the ghost whisked out of the leg of his trousers. With that, the *Cigire* snatched up his briefcase and dashed from the room, shouting and huffing and puffing. We looked out of the window and could see the *Cigire* racing to his car, with the ghost spinning round his head – snapping and shrieking all the time. We laughed and laughed. Teacher laughed too. When the *Cigire* had gone in his car, the ghost whizzed back into the glass jar, where it gurgled and chuckled to itself. Patrick put the ghost on the Nature Table in our classroom for the rest of the day.

# THE MAY RUN
*Michael Scott*

May Day, the ancient Celtic festival of Beltane, a time of magic and mystery, when old rituals and curious customs are performed.

Kevin O'Neill took a deep breath and attempted to calm his pounding heart. Wrapping his arms tightly around his chest, he tucked his fingers into his armpits, and stamped his feet against the cold, bare feet squeaking on the dew-damp grass, water droplets splashing his knees and thighs.

Looking down, Kevin rubbed a toe in the ankle-high grass. The heavy dew would make the run more difficult, though he knew his sisters would be pleased. Last night he had listened to them planning to sneak out of the cottage to gather the dawn dew. He had laughed at the ancient superstition that the dew on May morning had special properties and could make a plain girl pretty and a pretty girl beautiful. He reminded them this was now the nineteen-twenties and that there was no place for such folklore in a modern Ireland. He'd shut up however, when Kathleen, his older sister, reminded him that the May Run was just as much a superstition.

The May Run. Every year on this day, the boys of the village would gather on the banks of Lough Gur to make the run; those who completed it would be considered young men . . . those who failed would spend another year playing with the little boys. There were some men in the village who had never completed the run. It was a shame that followed them into adulthood.

Well Kevin wasn't going to fail. He was going to prove his courage and finish the run . . . even though he was terrified. Taking a deep breath, he attempted to calm his fluttering stomach.

"Ready?" The voice of one of the older boys hung flat and expressionless on the chill air. The eight boys gathered along the edge of the path nodded and murmured their readiness.

"O'Neill, you'll run first."

Kevin nodded quickly, hiding his disappointment. The first run was always the hardest and the runner would then have to stand in icy clothes while the rest of the boys took their turn.

"You know what to do?"

Kevin nodded again.

"Go!"

Kevin ran. The boy's dark eyes ranged over the uneven ground, deliberately concentrating on it, trying not to think about anything else as he pounded towards the lake, bare feet splashing through the dew-damp grass, nettles and razor sharp blades stinging and biting at his flesh, though he felt no pain. His staring eyes fixed on the silvery surface of Lough Gur. The water was quite opaque beneath the sunless sky, looking like a sheet of lightly polished metal. His bare feet touched the muddy verge of the lake. Now for the hard part; he had to throw himself into the water.

No one knew when the ceremony had begun. His father told him that it was left over from pagan times, when criminals were sacrificed to the dark lake spirits. His mother told him that Patrick had baptised local people in the lake's cold waters, and that's how the ritual started.

Wet pebbles and sharp stones bit into his feet.

The lads who had gathered to observe this rite of passage grinned wickedly and elbowed one another. They had all done this and knew what Kevin was about to experience: the heart-stopping chill of the water, the aching muscles, then the long shivering walk back home and, if you were particularly unlucky, you caught a cold afterwards and spent the best part of a week coughing and sneezing in bed.

The boys of the village had been jumping into Lough Gur on May morning for as long as anyone could remember. Whatever ancient legends were associated with the water, one particular story was told again and again, and was given as the reason why the boys braved the water.

The mighty Earl of Desmond had been notorious in the sixteenth century for his practice of dark magic. He had brought shame to his proud and ancient name of Fitzgerald, and struck terror in the heart of the local people. It was commonly believed that he was a shape-changer, able to take on the form of any bird or animal at will.

When the man known to many as Wizard Fitzgerald finally died, there were those who said it was a hoax, that he could not die, that he had made an unholy pact with the devil to preserve his foul life forever. Some of his family tried to claim the stories about him were nothing more than rumours put about by his enemies, but the ordinary people would not listen. Tales of his spectral form were soon being told throughout the south and west of Ireland. Many of the stories faded and were forgotten, but one remained: the Wizard's May morning ride.

Once every seven years, on the first day of May, it was said that the immortal Wizard emerged from beneath the waters of Lough Gur. Wearing full armour, on the back of a huge warhorse, he would gallop across the surface of the lake. And the only evidence of the spirits passing would be the splashes from the horses magical silver hooves etched into the still waters of the lake. Legend had it that the wizard would be forced to repeat this performance time and again until the horseshoes wore so thin that they fell off . . . but since water has no effect on silver, he was bound to ride for all eternity.

However, at some time in the past, the young lads of County Limerick had decided that the lake was perfect for a rite of passage from boyhood into manhood. On the first of May the boys would gather on the lakeside, run into the water and duck their heads beneath the surface, proving their courage. On most years, the run was accompanied by shouts and cries and echoing laughter, but on the seventh year the run was invariably conducted in absolute silence.

And this was a seventh year.

Ice water splashed over Kevin's toes, and he slowed. He was supposed to throw himself in just as Wizard Fitzgerald was expected to rise from the waters. And just because the wizard hadn't risen from the water in the past didn't mean that this couldn't be the very morning . . .

Kevin measured his steps to the water's edge. Six, seven at the most.

Beyond the lake stood a remarkable, and ancient, stonework. In a time beyond the known history of Ireland, an earlier race had erected numerous stone circles around the country, testifying to ancient and sometimes bloody rituals. The largest of these stood beside Lough Gur. Aligned with the stars and the seasons, it might once have served as a calendar. According to one local legend however, its purpose had been human sacrifice, and it was the aura of these dark deeds that still lurked in the stones and held the wicked Earl of Desmond in the waters of Lough Gur.

*Four steps* . . .

It was a good story. The boys gathered on the lake shore didn't quite believe it . . . but they weren't sure if they disbelieved it either.

*Two* . . .

At the very last moment, Kevin thought he saw movement just below the surface of the lake in front of him. He tried to stop, but by then his momentum was too great.

*One* . . .

With a despairing wail quite unlike the courageous

yell he meant to give, he plunged into water. The icy water hit him in the pit of the stomach like a solid blow, robbing his breath, numbing feet and legs. He stumbled and fell forwards, splashing and kicking, but managed to stay upright. If he had been able to get a good purchase with his toes in the mud, he might have turned back then and scrambled ashore. He was a good swimmer and didn't fear the water. But the mud was old, slick ooze. His foot skidded and slipped and he lurched sideways, arms flailing, then he suddenly disappeared beneath the surface. The watching boys on the lake shore laughed and shouted and yelled at the spectacle.

Kevin came spluttering to the surface. He spat out a stream of lake water. A sense of elation flooded through him. He was in the lake, he was alive, he had actually gone under and come up again. No wizard had appeared, no hand had snatched him down.

He had made the May Run: he was a man.

The boy turned and began to make his way back towards the shore – that's when the idea came to him. He was waist-deep in the water, smiling triumphantly, when he suddenly flung up his arms again and screamed convincingly. "Something's caught me. A hand! There's a hand on my ankle!" he cried, his voice rising. He ducked beneath the surface, waited a moment, then came up again. "Help me," he screamed, and ducked under again, doubled over in the cold water.

The boys on the shore exchanged startled glances, suddenly unsure. It wouldn't be the first time a trick like this had been played, and everyone who played it thought they were the first. But the screams sounded so convincing . . . They looked at one another, unsure, uncertain, unwilling to make the first move.

While they struggled with their consciences, Kevin, remaining below the lake's mirrored surface, struck out towards the left, swimming blind. If they came in for him he would not be where they thought. And he would have the last laugh, sitting on the shore, watching the older boys getting their good clothes wet, whereas he had been careful to wear his oldest, shabbiest clothing.

"Kevin?"

"Kevin? Where are you?"

"Kevin!"

In a group, the boys raced down into the shallows, Kevin's name ringing hollowly on the still morning air. The bitter chill of the water stopped their rush and they waded cautiously into the lake, staying very close together, and began feeling around under the water, its surface now cloudy with mud and silt, trying to catch hold of their friend's arm or shoulder. Keeping in a ragged line, they moved further and further from the shore, icy water creeping up past ankles and knees, then thigh high.

When he could hold his breath no longer, Kevin allowed himself to float to the surface. Brushing water from his eyes, he was surprised to discover how far he'd come. His friends were thirty or forty paces away, standing waist-and shoulder-high in the water, white-faced with panic, calling his name and taking great gulps of air before they ducked down to try to find him on the lake bottom.

Crawling up onto the bank, he pushed his sodden hair back off his forehead, climbed to his feet and was raising his arm to call them, when he saw it . . .

A ripple.

A bubbling disturbance out in the centre of the lake.

A perfect ripple that spread in an almost perfect circle. A gleaming metal helm broke the surface, its slitted grill evil and menacing.

Kevin's screamed warning died in his throat.

The Great Wizard rose up from the dark depths in one tremendous thrust, holding a sword above his head as if he had used it to cleave the water. Lake water streamed off his metal armour like quicksilver, weed from the bottom of the Lough festooned his shoulders and hung across his armoured chest like a great slimy cloak. The ornate armour was dappled and speckled with rust and mildew like some foul disease.

His horse was a chestnut stallion almost the colour of blood. Caparisoned in the fashion of the sixteenth century, with the earl's faded and rotted colours, the animal leaped upward from the lake and drew air into its nostrils with a tremendous snort.

Kevin screamed.

The other boys turned, startled, and looked toward him. But their reactions were too slow. All their surprise was focused on seeing him alive and well. They thought his outstretched arm and wildly pointing finger was directed towards them. They did not see the Great Wizard galloping silently, terribly, toward them across the surface of the lake, the horse striking silver sparks from the water.

The earl rose in his stirrups and swung his sword.

With an ear-splitting scream, Kevin threw himself backwards and ran off across the dewy meadow, slivers of grass cutting into his legs, nettles stinging his feet. He heard shouts, cries . . . but the noises were faint and distant, drowned out by his thundering heart. He fell close to the edge of the road and tumbled over, sliding back off the wet grass, slipping back towards the water. He dug his fingers into the soft soil and pulled himself to his feet and glanced back.

There was no sign of the Wizard or the horse – or the boys. No sign that they had ever existed. The surface of Lough Gur was disturbed only by the wind, ruffling it into tiny wavelets . . . and by the spreading pool of crimson that floated intact for a little time before it was dispersed by the waves.

Kevin O'Neill never regained his senses and although he lived on into the middle of the twentieth century, he was never able to speak of what he saw that day.

The other boys were never found.

And the Wizard still rides the lake once in every seven years.

# THE PENNY WHISTLE
*Mary Regan*

"I suppose you get what you pay for," his mother said as she surveyed the house; a long, low, one-storied building with various odd bits added on to one end. Green stains crept up the dirty-white walls and flakes of loose plaster littered the windowsills. A few straggly trees protected the house from sea winds but there wasn't another sign of life to be seen for miles around.

"At least we're near the beach," said Matt. "Come on you two," he shouted to his sisters who stood silently staring at their bleak surroundings, their eyes wide with unease. "Give me a hand to get this stuff inside." He began to haul the bags towards the door and his mother turned the key in the lock.

It was difficult to adjust to the gloom inside after the bright sunlight outside but slowly the layout of the room became visible. It was quite big but very sparsely furnished with a table, four kitchen chairs and a sagging sofa. Flitters of lace curtains drooped from the only window and the large open fireplace was cold and empty.

"This place hasn't seen many changes over the years," said his mother grimly, "but there's running water at least, thank God." She turned on the tap at the old delph jawbox behind the door and a rush of treacle brown water splurted out.

"Yuck!" cried Anne and Deirdre in unison.

"It's only the colour it gets from coming through the bog; it's clean enough," their mother soothed. "Sure look – it's grand now." The flow of the water had slowed and now it was a pale golden brown. "I'll get a fire going here to cheer us up," she said. "You lot start unpacking."

Matt felt a pang of pity for his mother; he supposed she had been ripped off. She had been determined to get them out of the city and into the fresh sea air and the ad in the paper read well – 'Old world cottage, authentic features well preserved'. Well, at least she had her fresh air and wide open spaces.

In a darkened recess beside the chimney breast Matt discovered a stairway; it was more a ladder really but it was made out of sturdy slats of black wood. He climbed up and found himself in a small room tucked up under the eaves. It was a sort of a loft and at one time must have been open to the kitchen as the separating wall was made of flimsy plywood. The room was furnished with a small iron railed bed, a brown wooden chair, a cupboard for clothes and a chest of drawers with a black-spotted mirror on top. One tiny window nestled under the beams that held up the roof. There was so little space up there that it would hardly be possible for an adult to stand upright.

"This is my room," he shouted down from the door. The girls came tumbling in from exploring the other rooms and their faces crumbled with disappointment when they saw what they had missed.

"That's not fair!" protested one. "He always gets to pick," complained the other.

"Tough luck, Zombies," smirked Matt.

"Matt, don't talk to your sisters like that," scolded his mother.

"There's a big double bed in the room below for you two," she decided. "Matt has to have a room to himself." The girls grumbled as their brother stuck out his tongue in triumph.

As he was unpacking his rucksack Matt noticed something tucked into a joint in the rafters. It was well up the arch of the roof – he could just reach it by standing on tiptoe. He pulled at it but it was jammed well in. He fetched the chair to stand on so that he could get a better grip on it. When he came face to face with the object he was disappointed to discover that it was just a dust-covered crockery bottle. It had a loop for a handle and the neck was stopped with a cork that was pushed right in so that nothing of it projected above the lip. He gave the bottle another push but he could not dislodge it from its position. Then he lost interest; it was only an old jar with no markings on it so he left it where he found it.

When everything was nearly in order and the fire was blazing up the chimney the cottage looked more cheerful and so did his mother.

"Now you lot get outside for an hour or two, I'll see about the dinner," she ordered. The girls ran ahead, noisy with excitement and anticipation, and soon they had turned off the roadway on to the narrow track that led down to the beach. Matt didn't run with them, of course; he stuck his hands in his pockets and walked at a more leisurely pace behind them.

He walked through a gap between high sandhills and suddenly he was on a huge beach of salt-white sand. Small children squealed in delight as they ran in and out through the sun-drenched waves and over to his left the sands came to an end and the rocks began. More children were scattered over the rocks but they were older – his age or more. Matt could see that Deirdre and Anne were already climbing over slippery seaweed and dabbling in rock pools. They're great company for each other, he thought to himself as he too went to investigate the possibilities of the rocks. He found a comfortable niche and sat down to watch a group of boys who were sporting themselves in a natural rock pool that was deep enough for swimming. The boys all seemed to know each other and they had equipment of every sort – wet suits, surf boards, diving gear and a small wooden boat with an outboard engine. Their accents were strange to Matt and hinted of posh schools and big detached houses with lush gardens. He sat for a while throwing pebbles into the water and watching the boys. Then he decided to go back to the house in case his mother needed some help with the dinner.

He walked up the lane kicking a stone in front of him. It was the first time that he could ever remember being away from the city except on school day-trips and he was feeling a bit peculiar. He missed the narrow streets and the back lanes, and the friends that had never been 'made' but just grew there the same as himself. He turned a bend in the lane and saw a figure shuffling ahead; it was an old man bent low over a walking-stick. His trousers flapped wide around his legs and his coat was dragged up at the back by the stoop in his bony shoulders. A small black-and-white dog, with short legs and a pot belly, frisked and trotted at his heels. Matt slowed his step. He didn't want to catch up with the old man. It would mean he would have to speak and he was no good at talking to strangers. But the man was going at an unbelievable snail's pace and in spite of himself Matt was gaining ground. Then the dog spotted him. It came towards him barking joyfully and leaping as high as it could on its stumpy legs.

The old man stopped and turned slowly round.

"Mind your manners there and stop that racket," he scolded but the dog ignored him. "He likes company," smiled the old man apologetically. "Come here, Napoleon. Behave yourself!"

There was nothing for it now. Matt would have to walk along with the old man.

"We don't get much traffic along this bit of road. Are you visiting?"

"We're staying along here – on holiday," said Matt. "We have that house just there."

The old man's bushy white eyebrows lifted in surprise and his blue eyes stared at the house which had just come into view. His slow shuffle stopped altogether.

"The old McKinney house," he said almost to himself. "I saw them dickeying at it and then the smoke today from the chimney had me wondering."

"Do you live near?"

"Th'onder," replied the man pointing with his stick towards a hollow on the other side of the road. At first Matt could see nothing but then a thin trail of smoke caught his eye. It was coming from a thatched roof that was sprouting grass and was well below the level of the road.

"Do you live there by yourself?"

"Me and Napoleon. Are you from the city yourself?"

Matt nodded. They were now at the front yard of his house. "Well, I'll be going then," he said and cleared as fast as he could.

Once inside he went to a window and looked out. The old man was standing motionless where Matt had left him. He was staring fixedly at the house. Very slowly he raised a bony hand and blessed himself. Then he turned and shuffled towards the spiral of smoke in the hollow. Peculiar, thought Matt to himself.

The smell of the dinner and the hollowness in his stomach drove all thoughts of the old man out of Matt's head until he was tucked up in bed that night. His mother moved about in the room below and he could see light through the chinks in his floorboards. He began to wonder why the old man had blessed himself before passing the house. He thought about it and thought about it until he tired his brain out and he drifted off to sleep.

Sometime that night Matt found himself wide awake again. The room was pitch black now and he felt strangely uncomfortable, not physically for the bed was fine, but inside himself. He felt he was in someone else's room and he had no right to be there. A desperate sadness oozed from the walls, the roof, the slatted floor and saturated the tiny loft room. Matt tried to get up but a powerful force clamped him to the bed. He wanted to call out but his voice was a prisoner too. Panic mounted inside his head. There was a presence in the room that was both pitiable and menacing and it chilled the warm flow of blood in his veins. "Please God," he prayed. "Make it go away. Please – whatever it is."

He held his breath and listened, for what he had no notion. Then he heard a sound. It was faint and in the distance but he knew that it was very threatening. The sound grew nearer. It was the tramp of feet on the roadway and the murmur of angry voices. A loud battering on the door of the house made his heart lurch painfully against his ribs. The door was smashed in and, in the room below, voices were raised in shouted threats. Screams of anguish rent the air and there was a great din of smashing furniture and breaking crockery.

Flames from many firebrands flickered in the darkness and his room seemed wide open to the light and noise. Matt wanted to rise and go to help his mother and sisters but he was still a prisoner of the invisible force. Footsteps rattled on the ladder and the voices grew louder. He slipped under the duvet until even his head was completely covered up. The angry shouting now filled the room and he heard the hauling of furniture across the floor. Bodies swarmed round his bed and, amid a vile stream of hoarse curses, Matt felt clumsy hands pull and haul at his bedclothes. The duvet began to close around him. Tighter and tighter it twisted and strangled until he was coiled up like a sausage roll. He was being suffocated in the downy folds of his own quilt! He couldn't move. He couldn't breathe. His brain grew numb. His senses dulled. The angry voices drifted away into the night and Matt was sucked into a black hole of nothingness.

A dull throbbing pain hammered in his head and Matt opened his eyes. He was still swamped in blackness but he no longer felt paralysed and the room was peaceful and silent. Gingerly he moved his head inside his cocoon and then he raised his hand and pulled the duvet away from his face. Daylight streamed in through the window and nothing in the room seemed to have been disturbed – except himself. He could have had a nightmare but he knew he hadn't. There was nothing fantastic about what he had experienced; it was real and brutal, but beyond explanation.

The tum-teasing smell of frying bacon drifted up through the floorboards and in no time at all Matt was in the kitchen making a bacon sandwich. He had come to a decision. He was going to see the old man before he spent another minute in that room. He knew in his bones that the same thing was going to happen again only the next time he might not survive. He had to know why the old man had blessed himself before passing the house.

He fed the tail end of the greasy sandwich to Napoleon who came to greet him as soon as he approached the grassy hollow and the tumbled down house. The old man was throwing crusts to a couple of scrawny hens. He looked at Matt for a while and then he said, "You're here on business then." Matt nodded.

There was the remnant of a low stone wall to the side of the house and the man seated himself on it. Matt sat a little distance away from the old man.

"What happened up there?" he asked.

"What d'ye mean?"

"In that house – something awful happened there."

With maddening slowness, the old man pulled a pipe from his pocket and filled it. When he lit it an acrid smelling smoke stung Matt's nostrils but the tobacco had a soothing effect on the old man and he settled himself more easily.

"There hasn't been anybody lived there for years," he said puffing steadily. "My grandfather told me about it when I was about your age. The McKinney house used to be a shebeen well over a hundred years ago – nearer a hundred and fifty now."

"What's a shebeen?"

"A shebeen is a drinking house; a drinking house that is outside the law. There were plenty of them around these parts long ago. Do you see those hills there? Well, there was hardly a cleft in the rock that hadn't an illegal still. The farmers hereabouts couldn't scrape a farthing from the land that didn't go into the pocket of the landlord and so they made the poteen up in the hills. There was a terrible tax on the legal whiskey and the ordinary folks couldn't afford it so they went to the shebeens where the mountainy poteen was cheap and plentiful."

None of this was throwing any light on the weird happenings of the night before but the old man was in the way of telling a story and Matt didn't interrupt.

"McKinney, who lived in the house beyond there, was making a tidy penny out of the poteen but he wasn't satisfied. He got greedy. 'Come back next week', he began to say to the mountainy farmer when he called to collect his dues for the poteen. But next week never came. So eventually the farmer confronted him and demanded payment or he would supply him with no more poteen. 'What is that to me?' said McKinney. 'Sure aren't the hills crawling with poteen makers all lining up to sell to me?'

'A debt is a debt', said the farmer. 'And it must be paid'.

'Then take me to court!' chuckled McKinney the wily old divil.

"You see young man, there could be no taking to court," the old man explained. "The whole operation was outside the law and if the farmer sought justice in the courts then the whole cartload of them would end up in the gaol. McKinney was very pleased with himself. He had made a right profit from the poteen and no bills to pay. He could try the same trick over again with the next supplier. But the farmer was not finished with him. He went back to his cabin in the mountains and he gathered his family around him and he told them the whole story. Now, although the farmer was a small weasel of a man, God had blessed him with four sturdy sons and they were not going to let McKinney get away with his cheating and his conundering. No, indeed they were not! 'If we can't get it in coin then we will take it in kind,' decided the eldest son and the four of them, and a whole rake of relatives, set off to pay McKinney a night-time visit.

Now, although McKinney had a great craving for money and wealth, he had one treasure that he valued above all worldly goods. That was his one and only child, a young boy of seven or eight years of age. By all accounts he was indeed a blessed child; good-natured, handsome, and touched by the fairies so that he could play the shee music on his penny whistle enough to steal your soul away. All day long he played that whistle until he brought smiles to sour faces and charmed the very blackbirds into singing in tune with him. Now it was said that the boy loved that whistle so much that it was never out of his reach. When he wasn't playing it in the day, it was in his pocket, and when he went to bed at night, he hid it in a secret place in his room.

Well, it so happened that the farmer's angry sons came on McKinney's house in the dead of night when nobody was expecting them. Their intent was to strip the house of all its furniture and possessions in lieu of the debt owed. It was not their intent to harm a living soul. They broke into the house and what goods they could lift they took with them and what they could not lift they smashed to pieces. McKinney and his wife screamed for mercy and forgiveness but the blood was up in the avengers. They smashed crockery jars filled with the poteen and they piled chairs and tables on their backs. They even rolled up the bedding and carried it off with them. When they got to their home in the mountains they displayed their booty for all to admire and when they unrolled one of the mattresses they found a child – a young boy beautiful as the dawn, and without a breath of life left in his body."

The old man paused here in his story, perhaps the tragedy of it all was too much for him. It was more than enough for Matt. The two sat without speaking a word. After a while the old man knocked the dead ashes out of his pipe against the wall and sighed.

"The McKinneys moved out of the district after that and the house has since changed hands many times. Nobody has lived in it for too long. It has been empty now this many's a year." He rose from the wall with a bit of a struggle and Matt realised that the visit was at an end. He too got up and prepared to take his leave.

"Mind you," began the old man as if in afterthought, "my grandfather used to say that the young boy comes back to that house every night looking for his penny whistle. He can't rest easy, d'you see, nor at peace with himself, until he can play his lovely tunes again. It seems that all he needs to be happy in the world beyond the grave, is that penny whistle."

Matt walked back to the McKinney house and he was deep in thought.

"Are you not at the beach on a fine day like that?" queried his mother as he turned into the cobbled yard. She was lying on a blanket on a patch of grass at the side of the house, enjoying the sun and reading a book.

"I'll go down later," he said as he escaped into the house.

Upstairs in his little loft room Matt sat on the bed and began to think. He knew now that his room was haunted by the unhappy ghost of the little boy so cruelly choked to death. And he knew that every night he would relive the same horrifying ordeal and maybe even come to the same end – unless! The idea leapt into Matt's mind and the more he thought about it the more he was convinced he was right. The grisly haunting would continue until the boy had his beloved penny whistle once again in his possession. Matt had to find it! He had to find the whistle and return it to the boy or he himself would be smothered while he slept!

But where was he to look? If the whistle was in the house at all it would have to be in the haunted room – the old man had said that the boy always hid it somewhere before he went to sleep – but the room was so tiny and bare that it would be impossible to hide anything in it. Was he being silly? Could a flimsy penny whistle, almost one hundred and fifty years old, still be in existence at all?

He had almost given up when his eye lit on the crockery bottle tucked into the joint of the roof. Of course! The very place! It was well hidden and *could* have remained in the rafters undisturbed for a long, long time. Eagerly, Matt hauled the chair into the centre of the room and began to push and pull at the bottle. It would not shift. Then he summoned all his determination and strength and with a mighty effort he tugged and tugged until his arms were almost torn out of their sockets. The jar came free with a jerk and he tumbled off the chair.

"Matt, what are you at?" called his mother from her patch of grass below the window.

"I tripped over the chair."

His mother seemed satisfied with his explanation so Matt turned his attention to the bottle. He gave it a shake and thought he heard a faint rattle inside the thick crockery walls. He examined the cork. It was tightly jammed and impossible to move. The bottle would have to be broken open. Using both hands, he raised the bottle high above his head and brought it clattering down on the stone windowsill.

"In the name of God what was that?" called his

mother's startled voice from the yard below.

"Nothing," called Matt. "Just an old empty bottle."

"Well for goodness sake be careful in there! You'll have the house tumbled on us and a fortune to pay when we leave."

A terrible stench filled the tiny room and Matt held his nose and closed his eyes. Then, very slowly, he opened them. There lay the whistle; its wood perfectly preserved in the powerful fumes of rough liquor distilled in mountain hideouts over a century ago.

That night as he lay in bed he held the whistle tightly in his shaking hands and pressed against his trembling lips. The duvet was pulled up under his chin and he was prepared for anything. At once he sensed the terrible presence in the room and, although he struggled to stay awake, his eyelids grew heavy and he drifted into an unnatural stupor.

Once again he woke suddenly to the blackness of the night and to the dreadful course of events that he had experienced the night before. He heard the shouting and the smashing of furniture and saw the flickering torches in the room below. Then the raiders were on the ladder and in his room. As he slipped down beneath the duvet he felt the rough hands at his bed and the feathery quilt began to swallow him whole. The lip of the whistle was in his mouth and he held on to it tightly as he smothered. A final vicious twist of the duvet brought choking blackness but, just before the deadly darkness claimed him, he blew long and hard on the whistle.

Immediately the threatening atmosphere vanished and all was still in the room. The rough treatment had stopped and no harsh voices cursed or swore. Wrapped

91

in the duvet, Matt listened a while and then he blew again, gently, on the whistle. A faint rustle disturbed the hush and, tentatively, Matt pushed aside the duvet and sat up. A few feet from his bed a white mist began to swirl and gather. Then it turned into something more solid, something real. A young boy of seven or eight, dressed in a rough linen night shift, stood by Matt's bed. His face was solemn but his eyes were open wide with excitement. Slowly he stretched out his hand. Matt placed the whistle in the cupped palm. The boy looked at it for a while and then a beam of pure delight lit up his small face. He placed the whistle to his lips, blew one long sweet note, and then he vanished.

Matt jumped out of bed but the room was empty, empty of boy and whistle, and empty of menace. He went to the window and looked out but the night was dark and he could see nothing. Then, faintly, from beyond the hill, he could hear the strains of music – music that sang of beauty and love and mystery and magic.

The next day the sun shone again and Matt swallowed his pride and went to the beach with his sisters. As they passed the grassy hollow the old man was at the road with Napoleon.

"Morning," said Matt. "Lovely day."

"It is, thank God. And it was a grand night too. I heard the whistling."

"What was he on about?" asked Deirdre when they had passed. Matt shrugged his shoulders in innocent bafflement.

"He's daft in the head, if you ask me," said Anne.

# THE STOLEN RING
*Gaby Ross*

T he trouble started when Dad decided to clear out the lily pond and found the ring. He was ladling out muck and dead leaves when a flash in the shovel caught my eye.

"Buried treasure, as I live and breathe," he said, picking it from the shovel and rubbing it on his jeans. He handed it to me.

It was a small gold ring with a large red stone set in little decorations, and it was beautiful.

"Show that to your Mum, and tell her it's her birthday present."

"He found it in the lily pond," I told her. "He's digging for your Christmas present now."

"Cheapskate," she laughed. "It is really beautiful."

"Come on, Mum. Try it on," I urged her.

But she gave a sudden shudder and muttered something about getting dinner.

We had dinner on the terrace, and after washing up, I was sitting there, just lapping up the ambience so to speak, when the ambience did something. It started with the sky, which went, if not quite green, then a very close copy, and the trees became closer, more real and brighter. Everything changed colour and looked the same but different. As if I was seeing them all for the first time. And there were no shadows. I could see right into bushes like they were lit up from inside. Even the grass was greener and cleaner.

I got up and walked slowly up the stairs. Mum was standing looking out the window.

"What is it?" I asked her.

"What?"

"The colours," I said. "The way the sky's gone all green and the trees . . . "

"You've had a long day, Poppet," suggested Mum. She thought I was delirious.

I decided to go to bed early and went back downstairs to get my book. I was rooting on the bookshelf when I heard a sort of rustling noise at the French door. Not very loud, like leaves falling or small things moving on the floor . . . I looked around.

I thought it was a rug at first because it was sort of browney-green, but it was moving, and bits of it came away and rejoined it, and then I realised. It was frogs. Moving across the floor of the sitting-room. In an army, hopping and slithering in from the terrace, in hundreds. I yelled for Dad and he came running in through the front door.

"Please, Daddy!" I screamed. "Please make them go away!"

He jumped aside, holding the front door open. Wide. They hopped forward in a fidgety tide and slowly started to go out the door. But there were still more coming in the French door, in uneven jumps and stopping altogether and looking around and then inching forward again, sometimes hopping almost over to where I crouched.

It took them ten minutes before the last one hopped tiredly away up the driveway.

"There's probably a logical explanation for this . . . " began Dad, but he had to clear his throat before he chanced speaking. Mum, standing behind him on the stairs, just shook her head.

I went to my room, but I felt edgy, and though I tried to read and listen to tapes, my room didn't feel right. I felt I was maybe being watched or something. In the end I got undressed in the bathroom. That's when Josh started screeching. I ran and found him on the landing, hanging weakly to the banisters, shaking and almost blue in the face.

"What is it, Josh?"

I knelt down beside him. He just shook his head and pointed to the wall by the stairs.

"It was coming up the stairs."

Mum and Dad came out of the sitting-room and he cringed against me, burying his face. They picked him up gently and carried him to their bedroom. Mum wrapped him in a duvet and held him close.

"He's had an awful fright, Conor," she told Dad.

"Maybe he's coming down with something," said Dad.

She checked his temperature. Subnormal.

Finally we all went to bed, but I left my light on all night. Nothing else happened, not that night. We never found out what the 'it' was that Josh had seen.

The following morning Mum went downstairs to start breakfast. I was only out of bed when there was a terrified screech – this time from the kitchen. We flew down the stairs, all except Josh, and in the kitchen – well there were mice.

They were everywhere – not just on the floor. They were on the counters and the cooker and in the sink. It was as if the kitchen was alive and moving, and Mum was standing, gasping with fright.

Dad picked up the sweeping-brush and actually walked through them and opened the kitchen door. Then he started to brush them out the door. He finally cleared the kitchen, but he was almost as white as Mum, and he had to clean off all the surfaces and disinfect the whole place because Mum would not go in there.

In the end I got breakfast ready and we ate in the dining-room. I went to school and Dad stayed home.

I met Esther Cullen at the gate and she asked what was wrong, so I told her. We'd just moved there, so I was new to the area and the school, but everyone in my class was dead-on, and I liked them. Esther told the teacher.

We had a long discussion about frog migration and disturbing mice and stuff and it was well after lunch when Kevin Hogan said about Lady Margaret. The teacher tried to shut him up, but Kevin was like a traction engine. You could switch him off, but it took a while before he stopped.

"Well, it could be Lady Margaret," he insisted.

"Who is Lady Margaret?"

"Who *was* Lady Margaret," he corrected me.

"Enough now, Kevin," warned the teacher. "Don't want to be giving people ideas, do we?"

"It's all right, sir," I said, lying better than usual. "I don't believe in that kind of stuff anyway."

"Very well, child," he said, settling himself in his chair. "Lady Margaret de Deauville was the wife of a wealthy Roundwood landowner. They were travelling on the Old Coach Road from their town house, when their coach was stopped by highwaymen and her husband was killed. They took all her jewellery, and tried to take her ring, which her husband had just given her for her birthday. She refused to give it and they . . . well, to put it bluntly, they chopped off her hand, removed the ring and left her among the bodies of the coachman, the footman and her husband. But she followed them and clocked one of the thieves with a rock. He fell to the ground unconscious and she retrieved her ring. She tried to find her way back to the road, but she was overcome with shock and loss of blood. They found her body the next morning. And the unconscious thief, who woke up, confessed, and promised to mend his ways, was denied the opportunity. They hanged him beside the Old Coach Road. Lady Margaret was buried with her husband in the graveyard opposite the Church. They never found the ring."

He paused for a moment and the class sighed in unison. Except me.

"A gold ring?"

"Yes, with a beautiful red stone in a very rare setting."

And we had found it. It was on Mum's dressing table.

"Isn't that a lovely story, class?" asked the teacher, with a long look at me.

"What about Lady Margaret?"

"Oh, that's just nonsense . . . " began the teacher, but Kevin got there first.

"They say she haunts the garden of your house, looking for her ring. 'Cos she still wants it back."

"But you don't believe in all that stuff, right?" asked the teacher.

"Right."

I couldn't wait to get home that evening. I wanted to tell Mum to get that ring out of the house and put it . . . I didn't know where. I just wanted it out of the house. When I got home, Mum was out shopping and she'd taken Josh with her, and left a note saying there was a snack in the fridge. I did my homework, stooged around the house, and ended up in Mum and Dad's room, looking at the ring on the dressing-table.

I sat down on the little stool and reached for it. Almost unconsciously I slipped it on my finger. It fitted. She must have had a very small hand before they . . . I shivered, but turned the ring on my finger. The ruby sparkled as it caught the light. I held my hand out in front of my face.

That's when I caught my reflection in the mirror, but it wasn't me. It had a face, this thing, blotchy and pale and staring straight at me from the mirror, not my face . . . an older face, full of hate, greed and anger. I backed away and almost fell from the stool. I tried to cry for Mum or Dad but couldn't form words. I put my hands to my mouth, but my left hand fell to the dressing-table with a dull thud. Without my arm. I could see it, my hand, lying there on the dressing-table, with the ring on the finger, my finger, and then everything went blank or was it black, and Mum's car door was slamming, and I lifted my hand and it was OK. The ring was back on the dressing-table. I fled.

I didn't tell Mum. It seemed stupid. We got the groceries packed away and Dad came in and we started dinner, and because this was Mum's birthday, I set the table properly in the dining-room, with candles and place mats. She likes that.

Dad's a great cook, the table looked good, the cake was nice, and it all went fine until Mum, I don't know why, decided halfway through that she just had to wear that ring.

It was a serious mistake. She slipped it on her finger, and let the candlelight play over the ruby and smiled down the table at Dad, who smiled back. Then her hand fell off. With the ring on her finger.

She gave a sudden gasp and fell backward to the floor. Dad rushed over, but she came round in a second or two and he helped her up. She gazed fearfully at the table, her mouth going like she was talking but she wasn't. Her hand was OK, just like mine was. The ring was lying on the white table-cloth, rocking back and forwards.

We cleared the table around it, and then I told Mum what had happened to me earlier. When the doctor came he sent Mum and Josh to bed and shook his head slowly.

Next morning, very early, Dad and I, we put the ring into a sandalwood box and wrapped it in a hankie soaked in holy water and brought it to the old graveyard. I really, really, really didn't want to, but the ring had to go where it belonged.

At the graveyard, there's a little gate with a sort of arch over it, and on either side, those dark green trees with the red berries. Inside it was quiet and you couldn't hear the traffic. A bird sang on the ruined wall of the old church, emphasising the silence.

We searched for ages, and found lots of Doyles and Byrnes and O'Tooles. De Deauville should have been easy to find, but one headstone looks much like another, no matter who's buried underneath.

"Maybe Mr Doyle is wrong," suggested Dad.

I doubted that. Mr Doyle was one of those teachers who is interested in everything and didn't get things wrong.

"Maybe there wasn't a headstone," he offered.

"Are you joking? The de Deauvilles were one of the biggest families around here. Why wouldn't they have a . . . ?" and we both guessed it at the same time.

"Because they would have a crypt," he finished.

It was right beside the ruined church. A biggish thing like a tool-shed only graver if you'll pardon the pun.

With an inscription:

*Lord Edward de Deauville*
*born 1772 died 1814*
*Lady Margaret de Deauville*
*born 1775 died 1814*

He went in and prised open the stone boxy thing and dropped the ring into it. When he came back out I handed him a hankie with more holy water and he wiped his hands with it.

We went home, got everyone out of bed, took out the frying-pan, and had a big fry-up out on the terrace in the morning sunshine. Mum put an ad in the paper, looking for a kitten. She does not like mice.

# THE LAST HAUNTING
*Cormac MacRaois*

Between the dark woods of Barnaculla and the Avonduff river lies a wide pile of rubble overgrown with briars and nettles. It is all that remains of Monashee House which was demolished to avoid further tragedy after The Last Haunting.

The late October sun had vanished behind the Wicklow Mountains by the time the five teenagers struggled over the ridge and saw the old hostel of Monashee below them.

"At last!" sighed Susan Burke as she eased her haversack off her shoulders. "I couldn't climb another slope if my life depended on it."

"Good old Danny," breathed Joe Lacey gratefully, as he lowered his plump body on to a convenient flat rock. "You said it would be there and there it is!"

Danny Moran grinned with pleasure. At seventeen he was the eldest of the group and the natural leader. The cross-country hike had been his idea and the choice of the abandoned hostel of Monashee for their first camp was his as well. He turned and looked back across Camaduff Glen.

Already a light mist was blurring its woods and hollows. It had been a long treck since the group had left the Wicklow Way and trusted in Danny to guide them to Monashee. More than once the faint-hearted, sore-footed ones had doubted him, especially fair-haired Orla Flemming, only now struggling up the slope, followed by Alan Rowan their permanent straggler.

"What's wrong?" asked Orla, her flushed face full of anxiety.

"Nothing, as usual," replied Susan airily. "We're here – almost."

"I told you I knew the way," grinned Danny.

"My head believed you but my legs didn't," grunted Alan. "Where is this ancient five-star hotel?"

"Directly below us," replied Danny.

Alan looked where Danny was pointing and saw a squat grey two-storey building beside a dark pine wood. "I can see why they abandoned it," he murmured. "It's so remote it's almost in the next world!"

"If we don't get down from here before it's dark, we'll end up in the next world," remarked Orla.

"For once I agree with you," said Danny. "Let's get on. This is the last leg of today's expedition."

"I'm already on my last legs," groaned Susan as she shouldered her haversack. "This thing feels like it's filled with rocks."

Danny led them down the slope. The descent was longer and harder than they expected and by the time they reached the bottom their legs were trembling with tiredness.

"If I don't get something to eat soon I'll die of hunger," grumbled Joe Lacey.

"Cheer up Joe," laughed Susan. "Think of the lovely slim figure you'll have by the time the weekend's over."

"What an imagination!" joked Alan.

"Not long now," Danny encouraged them as they climbed over an old dry stone wall. They found themselves on a rough track that curved downwards between two banks of ash trees supported by walls of mossy boulders.

"Look!" whispered Susan. "There on the path."

A large dog-like creature was standing in the middle of the track, staring at them. Its rust-coloured coat looked dull and untidy and its eyes were fearful and wild. Even as they watched, it turned and vanished into the shadows.

"What was that?" asked Orla.

"An old fox," suggested Danny.

"If it was, it was unusually large," murmured Alan.

"Whatever it was, it's gone now," said Danny. "Come on. We're nearly there."

Soon they turned a corner and there was the hostel right in front of them at the top of a small rise on the other side of a wide swirling stream. A row of well-worn stepping-stones invited them to cross.

"Going to Monashee?"

The voice was so unexpected that everyone jumped.

A thin bent figure detached itself from the wall below the ash trees and shuffled towards them as if part of the wall had come to life. They saw a wrinkled old man leaning on a stick. He wore a crumpled brown suit frayed at the cuffs and collar. His untidy hair and beard were an odd mixture of ginger and grey and his eyes gleamed like polished amber.

"Are you going to Monashee?" he repeated in his strange harsh voice.

"Yes we are," replied Danny, feeling annoyed at being challenged unexpectedly.

The old man stared at him for a moment. "It would be better not to," he croaked, shaking his head.

"Why not?" demanded Alan, moving towards the front of the group to stand beside Danny.

The old fellow raised his head, stretched out his neck and sniffed at him. "Not everyone who goes up comes down," he added mysteriously. Then he turned stiffly and limped towards an open gateway on their right, mumbling to himself.

"Who on earth was that?" whispered Orla.

"Some old sheep-farmer," replied Danny. "Probably been living on his own for too long. Come on."

As they stepped from stone to stone across the bubbling water they heard his voice calling after them. "Don't open any doors!" he croaked, then burst into a fit of coughing that sounded like a series of harsh barks.

Once across the stream they climbed the slope to the front of the hostel. The house, with its locked door and boarded-up windows looked cold and unfriendly.

"I can't believe we're really going to spend the night in that gloomy heap," muttered Orla with a shiver.

"Would you rather spend it out here?" retorted Danny.

Joe Lacey trudged up to the heavy front door and

pushed. It remained firmly shut. The leaves of a shrub that had obviously taken root in the hallway were pressed against the glass of the fanlight as if the plant was struggling to escape. Carved in the granite lintel above the door was the date 1840.

"Really creepy," muttered Joe. "What did that old fellow mean by '*Not everyone who goes up comes down*'?"

"Oh come on!" exclaimed Alan Rowan. "We're not going to let the ravings of a bewildered sheep-farmer prevent us from enjoying our first night's camping. We have food, sleeping-bags, fuel for a fire and ready-made shelter. Let's get inside and enjoy ourselves."

"Good man Alan!" agreed Danny. "Let's find a way in."

"'*Don't open any doors*'," muttered Orla but the others had moved away.

The downstairs windows were boarded up but they found one from which the boards had partially fallen away and Danny and Alan easily pulled the rest out so that everyone was able to climb through.

Once inside they switched on their torches. They were in a high-ceilinged room with a huge marble fireplace at one end. There was a dust-covered table with two chairs lying on their sides. At the far end of the room, a tall window covered in green algae and bird droppings let in a gloomy light.

"What luxury!" exclaimed Alan.

"It'll be dry," said Danny. "Let's get a fire going and fry up some grub."

Danny and Joe Lacey set up the two primus stoves and organised the food. Susan took the kettle down to the stream and Orla and Alan ventured into the woods to gather fuel for their fire. By the time they got back it was quite dark and the first drops of rain were beginning to fall. As Alan handed the last of the firewood in through the window to Orla, he heard a bark behind him. He turned and thought he saw a pair of amber eyes on the far side of the stream. Even as he stared at them they blurred into darkness so that he wasn't sure if they'd really been there. "Imagination!" he muttered and scrambled hurriedly through the window.

Alan had brought newspaper and firelighters with him and before long the pine twigs were cracking and hissing in the flames. Orla set candles on the mantelpiece and on the floor to spare their torch batteries.

By the time everyone was tucking in to juicy sausages, mopping up beans with thick white bread and gulping hot sweet tea, they were all in much better spirits. The rain was battering the windows and the wind whistling through the boards but their fire was bright and warm and everyone felt snug and satisfied.

"This place was a brilliant idea, Danny," said Susan and everybody agreed.

"When I was a kid in the scouts we used to tell ghost stories around the camp-fire," sighed Joe. "I was always afraid to go to sleep."

"That's a great idea," chirped Susan. "Come on Danny. Let's have a scary story."

"Oh, I don't know," Danny hesitated.

"Ah go on," coaxed Susan. "There's got to be a good yarn about a place like this."

"There is a story," Danny admitted. "I suppose I ought to have told you about it before bringing you here. The truth is that this hostel was abandoned because it's haunted."

He paused to take a mouthful of tea but no one spoke. The wind moaned in the chimney and the fire crackled. Realising he had a ready audience, Danny dropped his voice almost to a whisper. "There's a room upstairs that no one can sleep in. Those who try it wake up screaming. The door is boarded up but sometimes in the dead of night strange lights are seen and weird noises heard. After a dreadful night when screams drove everyone from the house, the Youth Association decided to abandon the place. That was back in 1940. They haven't used it since."

"1940," muttered Orla uneasily. "That was exactly a hundred years after the place was built."

"Yeah. Ghosts love celebrating centenaries!" chuckled Alan. "Pull the other one Danny. I bet you never heard anything here except other people's stories."

"That's true," agreed Danny with a regretful grin, "but it does have a rather peculiar history."

"Tell us," urged Susan, who loved being scared.

"The house was built by a landlord called Stoney Byrne," continued Danny. "He got the name because he owned quarries up towards Glendalough and because people said his heart was made of stone. One night during the famine when the wind was howling around the house and the rain pelting on the windows, a red-haired woman with a baby in her arms knocked on the door. She was dying of hunger and begged for a crust of bread and permission to sleep in the stables. When the servant girl brought the message to Stoney he flew into a rage and sacked the girl on the spot for disturbing him. Then he rushed out and drove the woman from his door with a horse-whip.

"Later that night, when he was in his bedroom, he heard a noise outside. He went to the window and saw the woman standing in the rain with her dead infant at her feet. She raised her arms to the window and cursed him and anyone else who ever slept in that room again. Then she collapsed on the ground, turned into a fox and picking up her dead child in her mouth, vanished into the darkness.

"Dreadful screams were heard throughout the house that night. In the morning when Stoney's manservant opened his master's bedroom door, a fox dashed out between his legs and vanished down the stairs. Stoney's clothes were lying on the bed exactly as he'd been wearing them but no one ever saw him again.

"Stoney's brother took over his estate but after one night in the bedroom he went insane and ended his days in a lunatic asylum. The house was abandoned after that. Eventually the Youth Association bought it and the rest you know."

"That's one hell of a story," said Joe Lacey in a dry voice.

"And that's all it is," added Alan. "Do you really believe all that stuff about a woman turning into a fox?"

"No," replied Joe, "but I wouldn't spend a night in that room and I'll bet you a fiver you won't either, for all your talk."

"You're on," replied Alan instantly.

The ceiling creaked loudly. Orla was sure she heard the sound of feet padding overhead. "Sounds like there's someone up there already," she said in a voice full of dread.

"It's only heat from the chimney causing expansion in the wood," said Alan. " Come on. Let's have a look at this 'haunted' room, that's if you're all not too scared."

"I'll go if you go," grunted Joe as he heaved himself up from the floor.

Danny led the way into the hall with his torch, the rest followed carrying candles. The front door was hidden behind the twisted limbs of the shrub that was growing up through the rotten floorboards. In the candlelight it seemed to writhe like a monstrous spider. The stairs were dark and forbidding. Danny hesitated.

"Up we go!" urged Alan placing a foot on the first step.

"No!" screamed Orla, making everyone leap with fright.

"For God's sake, what's wrong with you?" demanded Susan. Orla's eyes were filled with tears. "'Not everyone who goes up comes down'!" she gasped.

"Get a grip on yourself!" muttered Alan. "Nothing is going to happen. Come on, you lot." He began climbing the stairs holding his candle high in front of him. The others followed cautiously.

There was a wide landing at the top of the stairs with several doorways off it. The haunted room was on their left directly above the room where they had made their camp. In spite of Orla's protests, Alan and Joe pulled away what was left of the boards that had been nailed across the doorway. Alan gripped the door handle and pushed. The door remained shut but everyone heard the sudden scampering noise inside the room.

"Sounds like there's an animal in there," muttered Joe.

"Are you sure you want to go in?"

"Certain," replied Alan grimly.

"Ooh!" giggled Susan. "Isn't it exciting?"

Alan stepped back, then suddenly slammed the heel of his boot into the wood just below the lock. There was a loud crack, the door shivered and moved slightly inwards.

"That's done it," breathed Danny. "If there are any ghosts in there you'll have scared them all away."

Alan pushed the door. It reluctantly creaked open. They stepped warily inside. It was just like the room downstairs. The ceiling was draped with filthy cobwebs. The wallpaper bore the ghostly outline of wardrobes and bunk beds long since removed. A burst pillow lay abandoned in a corner. The floor was covered with an undisturbed layer of dust.

"There you are," said Alan. "No wild animals, no ghosts, nothing at all."

The door creaked behind them. There was a sound of footsteps on the stairs. Danny strode to the door and shone his torch into the darkness. There was nothing there.

"Let's go down again," suggested Orla.

No one objected.

The downstairs room was cosy with its fire and the remains of their meal but the shadow of the room upstairs lurked in all their minds and the cheerfulness had gone out of the evening. When the time came for Alan to go up again no one else was willing to join him.

Orla begged him not to go but he felt he couldn't back out without losing face.

"Have that fiver ready for me in the morning," he said to Joe as he headed off with his sleeping-bag.

The others listened to his footsteps on the stairs and then to the sound of him moving about in the room over their heads. As they settled down to sleep they heard Alan's voice shouting "Good night chickens!" Then there was silence.

The torches were switched off and the candles blown out. They lay in the darkness listening to the wind lamenting around the house until sleep overcame them. Only Orla lay awake hour after hour torturing herself with imaginings until even she dozed off at last.

When she opened her eyes again it was still dark. She had no idea how long she had slept. She lay very still, listening, wondering what had wakened her. Then she heard a snuffling sound at the door, a scratching as if a dog wanted to come in. The stairs creaked step after step as if someone was going up. Was it Alan moving about? She listened, not daring to breathe. Footsteps padded lightly across the ceiling. It must be a dog – or a fox!

Orla pushed up in her sleeping-bag and reached for her torch. As her fingers closed around it she heard a baby crying. Then she felt the whole house shudder. A shower of plaster fell from the ceiling like an indoor snowfall. The room was lit by a blinding flash followed by a thunderclap so loud it hurt her ears.

Everyone was sitting up now, struggling out of sleeping bags and switching on torches. The floor trembled under them while a great noise rumbled through the house. As they got to their feet they heard the most dreadful sound of all – a long terrified scream that made the hair stand up on the back of their necks. A series of thuds and crashes shook the ceiling as if a fierce struggle was going on overhead. Then Alan's voice screamed again.

Danny dashed into the hallway and the others followed. They raced upstairs. Alan's door was locked again. They banged frantically on it.

"Alan! Alan! What's wrong? Open the door!" shouted Danny.

The screaming changed to a lonely wail.

Danny and Joe charged the door with their full weight. It collapsed before them and they staggered into the room.

Alan was sitting quietly on his sleeping bag. Sweat dripped from his white face and his eyes were staring.

"Alan!" whispered Orla. "Are you all right?"

He looked at them in surprise. "I had a most peculiar dream," he murmured. He said nothing else.

They brought him downstairs. He sat in a daze on the floor while they made a pot of tea. The house was deathly silent. Outside a bird twittered at the first light.

"What happened?" Susan asked.

"A most peculiar dream," Alan mumbled to himself. "Drowning in the sea. It wasn't water. It was hair – red hair. Everyone is so hungry."

Danny poured a mug of tea. Orla turned to reach it to Alan but her arm froze in mid air. "Oh my God!" she cried.

As the light increased in the window Alan began to fade. Already they could see right through him and even as they watched he vanished completely. They were still gaping open-mouthed when the wailing began again upstairs.

Up they went again, slowly, fearfully. Alan was sitting on his sleeping bag. "I had a most peculiar dream," he murmured.

They brought him downstairs. This time his face looked older and his hair was streaked with grey. "So hungry," he murmured as he started to fade again. Upstairs the wailing began once more.

"What are we going to do?" sobbed Orla.

"I don't know," groaned Danny as he strode out into the hallway with the others behind him.

They didn't go up. Alan was at the door of the room. His eyes were wild and his mouth was wide open. As he stared down at them a terrible howling escaped from him. Then he drifted across the landing without using his legs and began to float down the stairs towards them.

They fled into the room and scrambled in a panic through the window without bothering to gather their belongings. Only when they were safely across the river and heading up the track did they glance back in terror at the house. Two foxes were guarding the front door.

# THE CHANCTONBURY RING
## Maeve Friel

They drove out of Brighton in the early evening. Chris sat in the back seat of the car, watching through the rear window as his last clear view of the beach and the town disappeared in a swirl of mist that had drifted in from the sea. They had come very abruptly to the end of the town and were already up on the soft rolling hills of the Downs when Chris saw the wooden signpost, pointing to Devil's Dyke. A shiver ran down his back.

Almost at once the road became a roller-coaster, plunging and rearing through whale-backed hills. The sea mist had followed them, dense patches of it nestling in the damp hollows of the hills or floating like ribbons of gauze across the meadows and on to the road so that Chris' father had to slow the car almost to a crawl. The white chalky soil, exposed in places by the roadside verges, gleamed eerily in the car headlamps. From time to time they heard the bleating of the solitary black-faced sheep that cropped the grass but otherwise the

Downs were silent. Moving through the empty countryside, Chris fancied himself watched by unseen eyes. There was something spooky about all this open space. Give him the clamour of the city any day, with millions of people all around him.

One hill, still far off, rose above all the rest. It reappeared each time they rounded a corner or reached the crest of a hill, until Chris found himself playing games with it, closing his eyes and daring it to be gone. But each time he opened his eyes, it was there, its distinctive silhouette crowned with a ring of trees. He could imagine it standing out against the sky, whatever the weather, watched by wary travellers.

"What is that hill called?" asked Chris, pointing.

"That's the Chanctonbury Ring," said his father. "It's a strange place, strange atmosphere. I climbed it once when I was a boy." He stopped abruptly as if he had just remembered something long forgotten and didn't want to go on.

"What?" prodded Chris.

"Oh nothing. I just remembered . . . " His voice trailed off. "It was an Iron Age camp, you know, and a flint mine. There are prehistoric kings buried up there. In my day there were even more trees at the top but they were destroyed in the hurricane a few years ago. The hotel we're staying in tonight is just below it."

The hotel turned out to be a big country house at the end of a long gravel drive. As his dad was signing the register, Chris heard raised voices and moved over to the window. A convoy of New Age travellers were driving up outside. Several ancient buses and lorries, their sides garishly hand-painted, were already blocking the road and a group of skanky-looking children were climbing all over the stone lions at the gate. Several hotel staff dressed importantly in tails and striped trousers were dashing about, flapping their arms and shouting at the travellers to be off. "There's no access through here for the public," one of them was yelling above the din.

"What's going on?" Chris asked the top-hatted porter who had carried in their luggage.

The man shrugged. "It's these crusties. They want to go up to the Ring for Midsummer night. Casting their spells and chanting and the devil knows what. The police moved them on from where they were parked for the last few days and have blocked the road up to the Ring. Nobody wants their sort round here."

"The Chanctonbury Ring?" asked Chris. "That circle of trees up on the hill?"

"Mmm," said the porter, "but it isn't called the Ring because of the trees. They worship the devil up there, make no mistake about it. It was in the paper. They should be locked up."

"What sort of things do they do?" Chris asked. That kind of thing fascinated him.

"Don't ask me." The porter's lips curled downwards. "If they had any sense, they wouldn't mess about with the powers of darkness. There are things up there best left undisturbed."

From outside came a deafening crashing of gears as another rusty old van roared down the path, scattering gravel in every direction. It drew up outside the window where Chris was standing and out jumped one of the strangest people Chris had ever seen. He – it – had long

117

hair done up in dreadlocks that were coming undone, and his whole face, his ears, his nose, his eyebrows, were covered in rings and studs. He wore a battered top hat, ankle-length coat and purple boots. As he jumped out of the van, his eyes met Chris' and he raised the bottle of cider he held in one hand and scowled at him, showing a mouthful of unwashed bad teeth.

Behind him a three-legged whippet trailing a bit of rope that acted as a lead dropped to the ground and began to scratch itself.

Chris jumped back from the window. "What do you mean, things best left alone?"

The porter sucked in his breath and shook his head from side to side. "I could tell you tales about Chanctonbury that would make your flesh crawl."

"What kind of tales?" Chris insisted. "Is the Ring haunted?"

"Haunted? I'd say it's haunted."

"Have you ever climbed to the top?"

The porter hesitated and glanced past the travellers' convoy at the hill beyond, the long barrow at the summit capped with a ring of trees. "Just the once, son, and I shall never go back. Some things are best forgotten and never talked about no more." With that, he picked at some imaginary fluff on the lapel of his red waistcoat and clammed up.

"Did you hear that, Dad?" Chris joined his father at the reception desk. "It's Midsummer night and there are devil worshippers here."

"Nonsense," laughed his father. "They're harmless. They just like to go up there because it is an ancient place. You know, Druids and Neolithic princes. I think

118

there might have been a Roman temple there too."

"That's right," said the receptionist. "People just have these half-baked ideas. Someone found a hoard of Saxon gold there not long ago so it attracts all these nut cases."

"The porter said they worship the devil," insisted Chris.

The woman at the desk looked down the drive doubtfully at the motley crowd of hippies and crusties milling about outside. "They chant, that's all, and walk around in circles."

"That's what I mean," interrupted the porter, coming over to the desk and fixing Chris and his father with a glare. "It's well known around here that if you walk around the Ring backwards seven times, Old Nick himself will appear. Don't go near it, that's my advice."

Chris' father laughed uneasily and turned away. Chris watched him replacing his wallet in the inside pocket of his jacket. He looked a bit jumpy.

"Did you ever do that, when you lived here?"

His father lightly touched his lips with his index finger. "No more talk of the devil."

After dinner, while his father sat over a brandy in the drawing-room downstairs, Chris returned to his bedroom and drew back the curtains. It was black and empty out there at first but then he began to see little lights flickering in the grass, glow-worms, he guessed, though he had never seen them before. Rabbits bolted across the lawn. There was the clatter of a bin-lid falling and a fox ran out of the shadows, looking back over his shoulder as if it knew it was being spied on. A pale full moon, with wispy clouds drifting across it, hung huge and naked in

the sky above him, with the Chanctonbury Ring and its
cap of beeches shining silver beneath it. The idea would
not go away. Chris took his coat from the hook behind
the door and slipped out.

The path through the woods rose steeply ahead of
him, the chalky earth gleaming eerily white in the
moonlight. To his left and right, lay dark secret places.
The only sounds were of water dripping from
overhanging branches and the occasional scampering of
small feet. Here and there, fallen trees blocked his way
and he had to scramble over them. They smelled damp
and rotten, their trunks covered in layers of yellowing
fungus like open oyster shells. After climbing for about
half an hour, the boy emerged out of the lonely wood on
to the spur of the hill. Far below he could make out the
lights of the hotel and catch a glimpse of the silvery sea
in the distance. Owls called to one another in their
strange unearthly wail as they came out to hunt.

A couple of hundred yards ahead on the summit of
the hill was the circle of beech trees. As Chris walked
towards it, he began to hear a dark humming which
grew steadily louder.

The New Agers were standing in a large circle
around the trees. Om, om, om, they chanted. They
began to dance, forming circles within circles, singing
to the pagan goddess Freya, praying for the renewal of
the ring of magic that surrounded the beech grove. The
procession moved among the trees, their dancing
increasing in pace, the male voices leading a dark dirge
while the women chanted over and over 'great and wise
is the spirit around us'.

Fascinated, Chris crept slowly forward towards the

moving shadows and lights among the trees and stood on the outer circle. Some of the dancers had left the main group and were tying black ribbons to the lower branches of the beeches. The chanting died slowly away and as the group moved down the hillside, the Ring ached with silence. On Midsummer Night you could believe anything might happen.

The earth beneath his feet seethed with life. He thought of all the people through the ages who had lived or worshipped at the Ring. He thought of the bones of all the generations who lay buried beneath it in ancient graves and fancied that they stirred and stalked the woods once more. Cautiously, he began to run, stumbling around the trees, anti-clockwise, slowly at first, then faster and faster so he was hardly aware of his feet kicking up the beechnuts and leaves that carpeted the floor of the woods. As he spun around, the thicket of trees on the barrow grew denser, darker, then faded away altogether until there was nothing left but a circle of saplings.

From the far side of the hill came the almost transparent figure of a young man. He was naked to the waist and weighed down by two enormous pails of water. Kneeling down, he began to pour the water around the roots of the trees, singing in a soft low voice. "I am Goring, who in 1760, planted the beeches on Chanctonbury," and his eyes met Chris' with a look so full of pleading or warning that, for a moment, Chris felt his cheeks burn with shame.

But as the image faded, his feet itched to resume their dance. For the second time, he began to spin around the Ring. A solitary red glow burned deep within the trees and he could hear raucous laughter. As he raced on, a group of men, staggering under the weight of a large wooden barrel, loomed up in front of him. Their drunken contorted faces leered at him as they passed, though their eyes were black and lifeless. Soundlessly, they laid down their ghostly load and began to dig among the chalky earth, the spirits of long-dead smugglers come back to Chanctonbury to bury their ill-gotten French brandy.

"Yes, yes, yes," cried Chris, possessed now by a force he could not resist, which snatched at him by the scruff of his neck and propelled him along the third revolution of the Ring.

Deep in the shadows, on the highest point of the barrow, something stirred. Wide-eyed, Chris slowed his pace but did not stop. A circle of men began to take shape, men with long white beards, Saxon priests, spectral in their long white robes. They raised their arms to the overhanging moon and bowed to the ground.

The fourth circle. Chris's heart was beating furiously within his chest but he was not afraid. He felt as if he had stepped outside himself, able to watch what was going to happen with objectivity. He was caught up in a game now that would not end until the last move was completed.

The ground beneath him shuddered and the whole earth seemed to tremble. Over the brow of the hill marched a column of Roman legionaries, foot-weary from walking along the straight paved road from the sea. They advanced along the spur of the hill and came directly towards him, passing clean through the trees to the left and right of him as if they were not solid at all. Chris smelt the sweet stench of their sweat as the ghostly column made their way past him towards the shadowy outline of a stone temple a little way off in a clearing outside the Ring itself.

For the fifth time, with the centuries peeling away like onion skins, Chris circled Chanctonbury. He hurtled recklessly around the mound, scarcely paying any heed to the squatting groups of stone-age warriors hammering flint stones among the chalky soil. He could not stop now. A strange dangerous compulsion led him on his sixth revolution. Sickened by fear, he was also excited by it, exhilarated by the dark spirit of the place, thrilled by each revelation. Wide-eyed, he stared at the raised mound in the centre of the Ring, the burial place of Neolithic princes, where a dozen skeletons now danced, their faces fleshless, their eyes sunk in deep sockets, their mouths hanging open to reveal the long teeth of their skulls.

And now the seventh circle. Chris stopped and looked around. Shadows and lights flickered among the trees and somewhere far off he could hear the last dying falls of the chanting as the New Agers moved down the hillside. The moon glided as if by stealth behind a drift of black cloud, plunging the Ring in darkness. Should he go on?

"Do it, do it," screamed an inner voice. "You've gone so far, don't chicken out now."

" . . . don't mess about with the powers of darkness . . . some things are best left undisturbed . . . " The voice of the porter echoed in his head.

"Do it, do it," commanded the other voice.

Chris took a few steps backwards. He felt tired now and frozen – and horribly afraid.

The moon slipped out from behind the clouds, throwing the beech trees nearest him into a pool of silver light. In the dark shadows behind them, something moved . . . A tall gaunt figure limped towards him. A man in a long coat, a long tail trailing on the ground behind him.

"Oh, God, no! help me, I didn't mean anything bad. It was just a dare," Chris prayed, throwing himself to the ground and shutting his eyes tightly like a baby does, as if blotting the figure out would make it really disappear. The footsteps drew nearer and stopped. Chris could smell him, a familiar appley smell.

"'Ere, boy," boomed a voice. "Seen my dog?"

Chris looked up horrified. His eyes took in the man's pockmarked face, the nose rings and lines of studs above his brow and in his ears. It was the crustie he had seen earlier, now stooping unsteadily over him, holding a bottle of cider in either hand. The dog's rope-lead dangled from his wrist. Without a word, Chris rose to his feet and hurtled towards the path back to the hotel.

Did he tell anyone? No. Whatever he saw up there, on the six circles that he made on Chanctonbury Ring, he will forever deny, even to himself. He will lock that night deep within his soul, never to be spoken of. As for what he might have seen, if he had gone on to complete the seventh circle, that is best left unimagined.

# THE DRESSER
*Mary Beckett*

Miriam was the youngest in her family – the youngest by a long way. Her brothers and sisters had all grown up and left home. If they had nothing else to do they came for Sunday lunch. Her mother made a huge meal and was happy. Miriam worked very hard to keep them listening to *her* news, because when they laughed among themselves she did not understand the jokes. She was quite happy all week without them. But on the road where she lived there were no other girls her age. As in her own house, the children had grown up and left. The parents who bought the houses still lived there. It was quiet. Sometimes Miriam's mother said that the whole district was tottering gently into the grave. Only Miriam kept her young, she said. People in shops downtown mistook her sometimes for Miriam's grandmother but they both laughed at that. The school holidays were long, though, with no children around.

So, when an invitation came for Miriam to a housewarming party in a new house on a nearby road, her mother said of course she must go. The invitation card was decorated with drawings of girls Miriam's age and was signed Selina Murdoch.

"You know where those houses are," her mother said. "You used to play on the site after they pulled down the lovely old house. It was really a country house with a big garden. The snowdrops and daffodils bloomed there for years afterwards. The people died. I don't really know anything about them."

"Lucy and Anne used to bring me round there," Miriam said. "They loved finding bits of china and ornaments and saucepans. They played house with their friends. I had to be the baby. When I said I was tired of being the baby they told me I could be the dog," Miriam laughed.

"After being in such a rush to knock down the old house the property people wasted a lot of time building those new houses. The site was empty for ages and when the houses were half-built I think the builders went bankrupt or something. Anyway, you'll go and meet this Selina Murdoch and tell us what the house is like."

"But I don't know her, Mammy. I might not like her. I have never seen her. She might be horrible. I don't know how she knew about me." Miriam threw herself into an armchair and then arranged herself with her head on the seat and her legs up over the back. "You're famous," her mother teased. "Everybody knows the lovely Miriam Garvey who wants to be alone."

So Miriam wrote her reply to the invitation:

*Dear Selina,*

*Thank you for inviting me to your party on Saturday afternoon. I am looking forward to it. I am sure we will have a great time.*

*Thank you again.*

*Miriam*

She took a long time over it. Then she went round to the new house and dropped the envelope through the letterbox in the heavy brown carved door. Miriam described it to her mother as being like the lid of a coffin.

"Goodness," her mother said, washing lettuce under the tap.

On Saturday morning her sister, Anne, called round to cut some sweet-pea. Her father said the more they cut, the better it flowered. Miriam told her about the invitation.

"Oh, I remember that place when they knocked down the old house," Anne smiled. "The things we used to collect as treasure! But you were very small, Miriam. You wouldn't remember."

"Not really, I suppose," Miriam agreed.

"Be sure and tell us tomorrow all about the new people. I think the houses they put up eventually were sold at an enormous price. I'd love to see how they are furnished," Anne said and her mother laughed.

"Oh, do you know what!" Anne suddenly turned going out the front door. "I brought home a little dresser from there. I had forgotten about that. A little wooden dresser with four blue-and-white plates left on it. I loved it, but I was afraid Lucy would claim it because she was

127

the eldest. Daddy used to call her 'the light of my life'. She got everything her way, I used to think."

"She says the same of you," her mother said.

"So I hid it behind the records in the bottom of the bookcase in the sitting-room. I couldn't play with it. Imagine! Wasn't I stupid!" Anne marvelled at herself.

"Like these millionaires who get people to steal pictures and hide them in their cellars," her mother said.

"Anyway, I've learnt sense," Anne laughed. "I must rush. Such a lovely perfume off these sweet-pea. See you tomorrow."

Miriam was already in the sitting-room kneeling on the floor, lifting out records half-a-dozen at a time. They hadn't been touched since her father had changed to compact discs five years ago. At last in the back corner she found the dresser. It was about the size of a medium hardback book. It was fairly well made but not at all valuable, her mother said. The four plates were crude enough, with smudgy blue flowers and birds in the middle and round the edge. Miriam looked at the underside to see where they were made. FOREIGN was printed in red spindly letters.

"It's nothing great, is it," she said, dusting it in the kitchen. "I don't know why Anne thought it wonderful."

"I don't know," her mother said looking at it with her head to one side. "It's pleasing, somehow. I think you should bring it round to give it to Selina this afternoon – unless you really want to keep it. In a kind of way I suppose it belongs to that house. First of all tidy away all those records and dust them as you do."

"Oh, Mammy," Miriam complained automatically,

but she liked reading the titles and by lunch time the press was tidy again. She put the dresser in a plastic bag although her mother suggested coloured wrapping paper.

"It's only rubbish," Miriam said. "I don't want her to think I'm bringing a good present." Then she began to worry that she really should be bringing a good present.

"Oh give me peace," her mother said. "Go and put on a clean dress."

The big, brown, coffin-lid door was open when she went round to the new house. The place was full of grown-ups talking and laughing and drinking wine. Miriam stood on the step feeling awkward until a woman called "Selina! Selina! Here's your little friend. Where is she – always disappearing. I don't remember your name, dear. Come on in. Maybe she's in the garden. Go on out there and look for her. Children should always be out in the sunshine. Orange juice or Coke, dear? Oh where is Donald? He should be here."

She shoved a glass of orange juice in Miriam's hand and went to the front door again to kiss the couple who had just arrived. Miriam could see no children. She was fairly sure Selina was still up in her bedroom. That's where she would be at this stage if she were Selina. However, she did as she was told and went through the huge conservatory, over the patio, past groups of men and women talking and laughing round a gas barbecue. Near the wall at the far end of the garden Miriam saw an old fuchsia bush – the ordinary wild kind she had seen on seaside holidays. It looked odd beside the perfect lawn, and garden centre shrubs that had obviously been planted only a short time. She thought she could sit down in the sun behind that fuchsia bush and drink her orange juice. She still had, under her arm, the dresser in the plastic bag. Maybe she would push it under the bush and save herself the embarrassment of it. But the plastic bag looked ugly there. Her mother objected to plastic bags caught on bushes and trees and high wires.

"I am so glad to see you!" She heard a woman's voice and she looked round to see who was greeting whom. At first she could see nobody. Then, below the bush she saw a figure about the size of a Barbie doll, but dressed in a blue-and-white striped dress like some of her mother's. She had a gold chain round her neck and a wedding ring on her finger. She had white curly hair and a face that was beautiful, though Miriam knew it was the face of an old woman. The wrinkles were still there, but they did not spoil the pink and white skin, nor the clear grey eyes. The tiny little woman laughed.

"I know you can't believe your eyes. Isn't that so? But I'm here all right. I've been here a long time, I'm sure. At least I've felt lonely. I *am* glad to see you. A good few people have seen me here, but they make themselves forget. They don't come back. A man came to fix up the garden to please the new people. He saw me. He was going to root out this fuchsia bush but I talked him out of that. We had a great talk about shrubs. I thought he'd come back. This was part of my garden, you see, when I lived here."

"Did you live in the old house?" Miriam tried to ask but it came out in such a croak that the woman laughed again. Miriam couldn't help smiling, because it was such a warm sound.

130

"Poor Miriam," the woman said. "You've had a shock. You came to see the new little girl and you find only the old woman who loved the house and the garden before you were born."

"Are you dead?" Miriam asked, although she had a notion it was not a question one should ask.

"I died before they knocked down the house," the woman nodded, not a bit put out. "They knocked down the house because I died. My husband died, and my daughter went to Australia and never came back, and my son died. My son was a painter. He died when he was young, but his pictures are still alive. Then I lived here alone, with nothing to love but my house and garden. I lived until I was old, and then there was no reason for the house to be left. So they knocked it down."

"Did you go to Heaven?" Miriam asked.

"Not yet," she said. "I'm not ready yet."

"What do you mean – not ready?" Miriam asked, curiosity killing all feeling of strangeness.

"I don't suppose you know the feeling because children are always lovely, always fit to be seen," the woman said gravely. "But did your mother ever say when a visitor came to the door, 'Oh goodness look at me. They'll think I'm always a mess in the house!' Or when somebody invites her out to a meal she wishes she'd had time to have her hair done? Or your big sisters, did they ever say 'I am mortified. I hadn't even on any lipstick!'?"

Miriam had heard all these things.

"Well that's the way I felt about Heaven. I just was not ready. I had to wait until I was fit to be seen." The woman sounded a little sad.

"You are very beautiful," Miriam said carefully.

"So are you," the woman said. "Your mother must love looking at you."

"How can you know about me or my mother?" Miriam asked, hoping that the old woman would say more pleasant things.

"I know a great many things," the old woman said. "A great weight of things. I see lovely things and good people but I also see people behaving so foolishly and I know the trouble they are storing up for themselves." She sighed and then, "But what are you going to do with that bag? I don't know what you have in it. Isn't that peculiar? A simple thing like that. I don't know what way my knowledge will develop – maybe I will know everything and find it good. But you don't want to hear the ramblings of an old woman – I used to say that, when I was old here."

Miriam was taking the dresser out of the plastic bag and the woman clapped her hands.

"Oh, it's Monica's dresser! Aren't you a good girl to bring it back here. I bought it for Monica, my daughter, when she was sick with measles. It was a horrible sickness for children. She was miserable. I bought her this in a shop that used to be near here. It cost half-a-crown. She loved it and played with it until she stopped having dolls. Even Michael, her brother, thought the little dishes were pretty and he was a painter, you know. It's a pity there are only the four plates left, but that is wonderful too, isn't it. Do thank your sister, Anne. But please, give it to the girl who lives here. Selina, her name is. People call their children the oddest names.

She is a painter like Michael. I know that, although I don't know her." Miriam was putting the dresser carefully back in the bag. "I love everything to do with the old house," she said. "Even a rough little object like Monica's dresser."

"You won't like the new house at all," Miriam said thinking of the white leather couch and big dark, glass-covered dinner-table she had glimpsed on the way through.

The woman laughed. "It's their house. Furniture is just to suit the people. They are not like me. The house is different from my house. But Selina will change things later on. It's time you met her."

"How will I find her?" Miriam asked, reluctant to take back the bag which was bigger than the little woman.

"Oh she'll come. I know she will. Then if she has the dresser I'll be able to come and talk to her. I've never been in the house." And at that, there was nobody beside the fuchsia bush except Miriam who felt herself suddenly to be very big.

She stepped out on the lawn and nearly knocked down another girl the same awkward size as herself but with light red hair.

"Are you Miriam?" she asked. "I'm sorry I wasn't down to meet you. I really am. I forgot what time it was. I was in my room and I had started a picture and I forgot the time. I was looking forward so much to you coming. There is nobody our age in this neighbourhood – isn't that right? Just you and me. It's weird, isn't it?"

Miriam put the bag-covered dresser in her hands.

"That's for you," she said. "It came from the garden

of the old house years ago. So it belongs to you."

"Oh what is it?" Selina asked but Miriam was looking at the paint on Selina's white blouse, quite a bit of paint, although the blouse had obviously been clean just before the party.

"Isn't that lovely," Selina said politely. "You are good to give it to me. I will draw a picture of it afterwards."

Miriam could feel herself blushing. Selina was not really interested in the dresser.

"Come on, do you smell the barbecue!" Selina said. "We have to see what we can get. We will be friends, won't we?"

Miriam agreed but she felt it was due to the little old woman to get the dresser into the house.

"Will we put this dresser up in your room first? Somebody might step on it here," she said.

"Is it an antique?" Selina asked.

"I don't suppose so," Miriam said and in her head she heard the warm laugh from the old woman. "But if you are going to draw it or paint it you would need to have it in front of you. You would hate to have to look for it all over the house."

"Oh all right," Selina said. "We'll just run up quickly. Or will I go by myself and you wait here?"

"No, no," Miriam said quite firmly. She wanted to see the house and she didn't want to be left alone again in this garden. As they ran up the stairs she took note of the white carpet and wine coloured walls and the chandelier in the hall. Selina's bedroom was pink and white but the counter under the window was covered with paints and pencils and pictures and paper.

"Can you draw?" Selina asked and Miriam said no,

quite happily. She was looking for a suitable home for the dresser. "There," she said pointing to a less cluttered corner. "Put the dresser there." She took it and put it in place herself, feeling she had found a niche for the old woman whose beloved son had been a painter.

Miriam didn't think Selina would bother being a friend to her so she enjoyed herself noticing all the furniture and decorations that were so foreign to her life. Miriam listened to the loud voices of all the grown-ups and stored up what they said. She made up her mind, as she often did, that soon she would be a nice kind girl. First, though, she would make her family laugh with her account of the party. But the beautiful little woman she would keep to herself, even though she might never see her again in this world.

# THE GHOST'S REVENGE
*Gordon Snell*

Philip was enjoying his first camping trip. Yesterday thirty boys and girls from the school, with two teachers, had pitched their tents in a sheltered hollow among the sand-dunes. As soon as the tents were up, they rushed down across the sand to splash around in the waves and the surf. At night they sat round the camp-fire and cooked sausages and sang songs and told stories.

Today, after another swim, some of them were playing volley-ball on the beach, while others were starting to dig a pool in the sand so that they could catch crabs and keep them there. Philip and a girl called Fiona had gone crab-hunting, Fiona one way and Philip the other. Philip walked towards the towering, rocky cliffs of Castle Head, at the end of the strand.

Perched right on top of the cliffs was the ruin that gave the headland its name – a castle built by the O'Neills many centuries ago. It was supposed to be haunted. No one could get to it, because the cliff path

136

which led there had crumbled away – but local legend said that on Midsummer night on the cliff you could hear a strange sound rising above the noise of the waves. It was like a fierce cry in a high voice that seemed to be calling the words: "Nine! Nine! Die! Die! Die!" over and over again.

Philip looked into the rock pools below the cliff. He could see no crabs – only seaweed, and a few crusty mussels clinging to the rock. He looked up. On the top of the cliff the tower of the castle almost seemed to sway, as the rolling clouds moved past it.

Philip felt giddy and looked down again. Then, just round the jutting rock of the cliff, he saw what seemed like the entrance to a cave. He stepped gingerly over the slippery rocks. He was right. There *was* a cave. He had to bend down a little to get into the entrance, but once inside, he was able to stand upright. He peered around in the darkness. He couldn't see how big the cave was. He decided that a shout might give him an idea.

"HULLO-O-O-O-O!" he called.

Then he gasped with shock. A voice just behind him replied softly, "Hullo there!"

Philip spun round. He could just make out a figure, sitting on a rock against the cave wall. As his eyes got used to the gloom, he realised it was a boy of about his own age.

"Wow! You gave me a fright," Philip said.

"Sorry about that," said the boy. "Not many people find this place. You can only get into it at low tide. Are you with the campers?"

"I am. We got here yesterday."

"I know. I was in the square when you got off the bus."

"Do you live in the village?"

"Nearby. What's your name?"

"Philip. Philip O'Grady."

"I'm Joe. How long are you staying?"

"A week."

"You'll be here on Wednesday then. Midsummer night. You'd better keep yourselves tucked up in your tents that night."

"Do you believe that story about the ghost?"

"Not really. But no one round here would spend Midsummer night in the Castle."

"You can't get into it anyway – the path's gone."

"There's another way. A tunnel leads up through the cliff, from the back of this cave. I'll show you."

Joe got up and went across the cave. Philip followed, walking carefully on the wet rock of the cave floor. They came to a narrow opening in the cave wall. Philip could just see some rough steps cut into the rock, leading up into total darkness.

"I wish I had a torch," he said.

"There wouldn't be time now," said Joe. "The tide is starting to come in already. It will fill the cave by the time we get up there and back."

"I'll bring a torch tomorrow," said Philip. "Will you be here?"

"Probably. I hang around here a lot."

"I'll see you, then."

But Philip's plans to explore the castle were blocked. When he told the others about the secret stairway in the cave, one of the teachers, Miss O'Driscoll, was listening. She and the other teacher agreed: it was too risky to go climbing in unknown caves. They must keep away from the place.

In their tent that night, Philip and his friends Darrell and Mikey talked about the stairway. They were determined to climb it.

"It will have to be at night," said Mikey, "otherwise we'd be seen going there."

"We could go on Wednesday night," said Darrell. "We might meet the ghost!" He made a spooky, moaning sound.

"Don't act the eejit," said Philip. "Anyway, I don't believe in ghosts."

"So you wouldn't mind going up there on Midsummer night?" Darrell challenged him.

"Of course I wouldn't."

"Right – that's settled. We'll go!"

None of them could back out now, though secretly they each felt a little bit scared.

When they told some of the others, Fiona said she and her friend Josie would come too. Soon everyone wanted to join in – or said they did.

"If there's more than six or so, they may notice we're gone," said Philip.

"Maire should come," said Mikey. "She does rock-climbing with her family."

So the six were chosen. They agreed that at half past ten on Wednesday night, they would creep out of their tents and meet on the beach. The moon was nearly full, so if the sky was clear they would have a good view of the castle.

Later that day Philip wandered down the beach

again. He was sure the teachers would be keeping an eye on him, so he didn't go round the corner of the cliff to the cave entrance. Instead he called "Joe! Joe! Are you there?" There was silence. He called again.

Joe appeared and stood beside the cliff, leaning one hand on it.

"Hello, Philip," he said.

Philip explained how they had all been told not to go near the cave or the secret stairway, and how they had planned the night expedition.

"Good," said Joe. "I'll wait for you at the cave entrance. I can show you the way."

"It isn't really dangerous, is it?" Philip asked.

"Not for me," said Joe. "And not for the rest of you, if you're careful. You're not afraid of the ghost, then?"

"No," said Philip. "I don't believe in them."

"You're a brave fellow. Like I said, no one around here would go up to the castle on Midsummer night."

"But *you* don't mind?"

"Not at all. I'm used to the place."

"See you on Wednesday night then."

"See you."

Philip and his friends lay in their sleeping bags, fully dressed. The moonlight slanted in through the tent-flap.

"What time is it?" Mikey whispered.

"Five minutes since you asked the last time," said Darrell. "Ten to ten."

The time seemed to creep by, very slowly, as the three of them lay there and thought about the expedition. There were no such things as ghosts, they kept telling themselves. There was no reason to be afraid. They all had torches. They would move carefully, and keep together. Everything would be all right. And what a story they would be able to tell the rest of them!

"OK," said Darrell. "It's ten-thirty. Let's go."

They crept out of the tent. Everything was still. The group of tents looked like a flock of odd-shaped animals, grazing in the moonlight. Down on the beach they met Fiona, Josie and Maire.

"This way," said Philip, and they followed him in single file along the beach. The waves sparkled as they lapped gently beside them. They rounded the corner of the cliff. The mouth of the cave was a hollow of blackness. There was no sign of Joe.

Philip went to the cave entrance. "Joe!" he called softly. "Joe! Are you there?" There was no answer.

They waited for a few minutes. Then Darrell said, "I guess your friend got scared after all, and decided not to risk it."

Philip was puzzled. Joe had seemed so calm and confident.

"He showed me where the tunnel entrance is," he said. "I can find it." He led the way across the rocky cave floor. The torch beams shone on the slimy surface, and on the clammy walls of the cave.

"Here it is!" Philip said. His torch lit up the first, uneven steps cut in the rock at the mouth of the tunnel. They led upwards into the darkness. They all stood there, gazing in silence.

"Are you there, Mister Ghost?" said Darrell, in his horror-movie voice.

"Shut up, Darrell!" said Fiona, giggling nervously.

There was another silence. Then Philip said, "Well, we can't chicken out now. Come on!"

He felt his heart beating fast as he took the first steps up the stairway. The tunnel was cramped and narrow, and he had to crouch down a bit. The air felt warm and damp. The stairs were uneven and cracked, and he had to tread carefully to avoid slipping.

After a while he said, "Let's stop for a bit, and get our breath." His voice echoed in the narrow tunnel.

"Suppose it doesn't lead anywhere?" said Mikey. "Suppose it's blocked up?" He sounded fearful.

"We'll just have to go back down again, won't we?" said Josie.

"Let's go on," said Philip. They tramped up the stairway, which seemed to go on and on and up and up forever.

Finally, Philip's head came up out of the tunnel and into a large open space. He looked around. He was in a wide room in the castle. The paved stone floor was patched with grass and moss. The jagged, ruined walls towered all around, with tall, empty windows through which the moonlight shone.

He called back, "We've made it." He clambered up the final steps, and the others followed. They looked around. The night was still. The only sound was the distant crashing of the waves on the rocks down below.

Maire went across to a window and looked out. The steep cliff was directly below, falling down to the battering sea beneath. "I wouldn't like to try rock-climbing down there!" Maire said.

The others peered over the window-ledge.

"I feel dizzy just looking at it," said Mikey.

Suddenly Fiona called out, "Listen!"

"What is it?" asked Josie.

"Mixed up with the sound of the waves," Fiona said, "I thought I heard a voice crying."

They all stood still, listening. Was it just the wind, Philip wondered, whistling through the cracks in the castle walls? Or did he really hear a high, sighing voice calling "Nine! Nine! Nine! Die! Die! Die!" He felt the hair on his scalp prickle. He looked at the others. They looked frightened.

"I think we ought to go back," said Mikey.

"Not till we've had a look around," said Maire.

"All right," said Mikey, "but let's keep together, OK?"

"Let's go this way," said Fiona. The others followed her across the floor, towards a gap in the wall. It looked as if it might lead to a tower that could be seen beyond the wall, pointing up into the night sky.

Philip watched them go through the gap, and was about to follow when he heard Joe's voice saying quietly, "Hello."

He turned. Joe was sitting on the ledge of the window – the one that looked down on the cliff and the breaking waves far below. How had he appeared so suddenly? He couldn't surely have climbed up the cliff. And if he had come up from the tunnel, they'd have seen him. Then Philip saw a low arch on the far side of the room. There must be a way in and out through that.

"Sorry I wasn't here to meet you," said Joe.

"That's all right. We found the way."

"Spooky old place, isn't it?"

"It is, a bit."

"Come on, I'll show you round," said Joe, jumping

down off the ledge.

"I'll call my friends."

"They'll catch up with us," Joe said. "That archway only leads to a blocked-up door in the tower. They'll turn round and come back here, and follow us." Joe went across to the low arch. "You go ahead," he said.

Uncertainly, Philip went through the arch. To his dismay, he saw that the floor dropped away steeply down a rocky slope. Philip lost his balance and stumbled and rolled down to the bottom. He sat up. He was on a grassy ledge of rock, on the edge of the cliff. If he had rolled a bit further, he would have plunged over and down into the sea below. He looked up. Silhouetted in the arch at the top of the slope he could see the figure of Joe, looking down.

"Be careful there," Joe said. And suddenly he was down on the ledge beside him. He was smiling. "Dizzying, isn't it?"

"Sure," said Philip. "Listen – the others will be wondering where I am. Can you help me get back up there? I think it's time we were going."

"Yes, before the tide cuts off the cave entrance. You don't want to be stuck up here all night."

"Tell them I'm here," said Philip. "Then if you'd just give me a hand to climb back up . . . "

"They can't see me," said Joe.

"What do you mean? Of course they'll see you. Call out to them!"

"They can't hear me, either. You're the only one who can."

"Don't be stupid. It's not funny."

"No, it's not. They think you've gone back ahead of them, down the stairway in the tunnel. They're all going down."

In the far distance, Philip could hear his friends calling his name as they went down the stairs: "Philip! Wait for us! Philip!"

He tried to call out, "I'm here! Wait! I'm here!" But his throat was tight, and only a faint croaking sound came out. They couldn't hear him, above the sound of the waves.

Joe was beside him again. He sat down on a large boulder. Philip was still sprawled on the grassy ledge.

"I must go after them," said Philip.

"All in good time," said Joe. "First, I want to tell you a story."

Philip had had enough of this practical joking. He lost his temper. "To hell with your story!" he shouted, recovering his voice. "I'm getting out of here!"

He got up and rushed to the bottom of the slope, but Joe stood there, blocking his path.

"Get out of my way!" yelled Philip. With both hands he went to grab at Joe and push him aside. But his hands grasped only empty air. Philip fell forward on to the slope. He sat up. Joe was back, sitting on the boulder, smiling.

"You can't hurt me, you see," said Joe. "No one can hurt me, not any more."

Philip felt as cold as ice. He stared at the boy in front of him. He looked as real as any of his friends. He stammered, "You're . . . you're . . . "

"I'm dead," said Joe. "That's right. I bet you never heard a story from a dead person before."

145

Philip felt faint. He could only sit on the slope and stare, and listen, as Joe began to speak.

"There were ten of us," he said. "Local lads and girls. Full of bravery, like you. We had heard stories of ghosts and Midsummer night noises. So we dared each other to come up here. We roamed around, exploring. It was dark that night – there was no moon. A storm got up. Everyone was frightened. We called to each other to go back down. Then I slipped and fell down that rocky slope, to just where you are now."

Philip edged away a little.

Joe went on, "I hit my head on a rock, and knocked myself out. They looked for me, I suppose, but couldn't find me. They decided to save themselves. They went down the tunnel and left me. When I came to, I clambered up the slope there, and started back down the stairs. I could hear the sea lapping at the bottom. I decided to go back up and wait for the tide to turn again. But a great rock fell and blocked the way. I was trapped, with the tide rising and rising – up to my feet, up to my waist, up to my neck. Above my head. I drowned, Philip. Right on that stairway you came up. When the tide went back, I was dragged back with it, and out to sea. They never found me." He paused.

"I'm sorry," said Philip.

"Sorry!" said Joe sharply. "Is that all you can say? I don't want apologies. I want revenge."

"On me? But I had nothing to do with it . . . "

"It doesn't matter. The others who were with me will never come here again. They've all left the place anyway. Ashamed of what they did. I want nine people to die in their place. Then I shall be happy. It's lonely, being a ghost all on your own. You should be honoured. You'll be the first to join me."

Philip felt panic rising in him. Ghost or not, Joe was mad. He had to escape.

"I'm not joining you! Never!" Philip shouted. He rushed at the slope, and this time Joe didn't stand in his way. He just sat back on the boulder, and began to laugh.

Philip scrabbled and grabbed at the loose rocks of the slope. His hands were cut and scraped, so were his knees. He kept slipping back as the rocks gave way. All the time, he heard the laughter of Joe behind him. At last, he scrambled to the top. There was blood on his hands, and his nails were broken. But he was back in the castle.

He ran across to the entrance to the tunnel, and began to go down the stairway. He had dropped his torch earlier, so he could only grope and stumble his way down through the darkness. The steps went on and on. Then he heard the sound of lapping water below. He went down a few more steps. His feet were wet now. He could go no further. The rising tide was blocking the tunnel.

He would have to go back up again, and wait above where the sea reached – wait till the tide went out and he could escape. He looked up. A dim light filtered down from above, so that he could just see the tunnel winding upwards. Then he saw the outline of a figure. It was Joe. The light seemed to shine right through him.

Philip knew Joe could not stop him, if he was brave enough to go onwards and upwards. He began to climb.

Then he heard Joe laugh – and there was another

sound too. A roar and a rumble, as a big rock began to thunder down the steps towards him. Philip crouched back. The rock crashed down and stuck, in the tunnel just ahead of him. He pushed at it with all his strength, but it wouldn't move.

He sat on the step below it. The sea was lapping around his ankles now. He tried to curl up on the step to get away from it, as if it was some creeping monster. Slowly, almost restfully, it lapped gently at his feet. Then it reached his knees. His waist. It began to lap around his chest. Soon it would reach his neck.

Philip thought of the crabs he had been looking for when he first found the cave. They were better survivors than he was. If he could only turn into a crab now, he could scuttle down the stairs to the sea and freedom.

As the sea came up to his chin, he pushed his head as high as it would go against the fallen rock. He gasped for breath. The salty water gurgled into his mouth. As the sea began to rise slowly, slowly to cover his head, he heard Joe's voice calling from further up the stairway, beyond the rock, "Good-bye, Philip. See you later!"

# THE CARACAL
*Eileen Dunlop*

"**Y**ou're a silly, hysterical girl," said the housekeeper crossly. "Strange feelings, indeed! This is a busy hotel, and we've no time to worry about chambermaids' feelings, let me tell you." But then she peered through her spectacles at Margaret's tear-stained face and added resignedly, "Well, I suppose you'd better take the rest of the day off. But – " her voice grew sharp again, " – be warned. If your strange feelings prevent you from cleaning room 27 tomorrow, you'll be sacked. Understand?"

Margaret nodded. She knew that Mrs Fowler meant what she said, and she knew that no one at the Caracal Hotel would be sorry to see her go. Ever since the day when she had lashed out at the ginger cat with a mop handle, causing the creature injuries which required treatment by a vet, the hatred in the cat's green eyes had reflected the hatred in everyone else's. They would laugh if they heard that she had been dismissed because she thought there was a ghost in room 27, but would also be confirmed in their opinion that she was crazy as well as cruel. They would be glad to be rid of her.

Margaret rode her bicycle down the drive and turned into the main road. It was a fresh spring day, with puffs of wind bursting among the trees and enough moisture on the air to cool her burning face. Half a mile further on, however, the countryside was swallowed abruptly by the redbrick mouth of the town, narrow streets edged with shabby shops and loud with traffic. Of course it hadn't always been like this, Margaret remembered as she waited in a miasma of exhaust fumes at the traffic lights at the end of High Street. Once the country road had meandered into the heart of the town, skirted by orchards and gardens thick with flowers. Instead of raising three grimy spires behind the brewery, the white cathedral had heaved its whole body into the sky, dwarfing the red-roofed houses which hung around it on the hill.

But how could she possibly know this? As the lights changed and the traffic lurched forward across the intersection, Margaret again felt fear like sharp fingernails at her throat. The answer was so simple, yet so impossible. She had seen it through the window of room 27.

Back at the flat which she shared in term-time with another student, but now had to herself, Margaret made a cup of coffee and went to lie down on her bed. She felt safe here, knowing that the door and windows were locked, and that the people whose red tabby cat used to haunt the hallway had moved to the other side of town. Slowly her tense body relaxed, and she was able to think without a suffocating hood of terror falling over her burning head. The story of the last fortnight at the Caracal Hotel began to spin itself out from a tangle of mad recollections. It was a story with a beginning and a middle but, as yet, no ending.

Margaret had been glad to get the chambermaid's job, because she had to supplement her student's grant to pay the rent of the flat during the Easter holidays. For a week, cleaning the first-floor bedrooms, she had been content. The Caracal was a newish hotel, converted from a country house built in the 1780s by Colonel Nathan Bewley, a traveller in the Middle East. There was a portrait of him in the hall, a wolfish, thin-lipped man in a white wig, dressed in a dark velvet coat and leaning on a rifle. Margaret had at first thought his face familiar, but after Mrs Fowler assigned her the attic bedrooms to clean during her second week, had forgotten him. The ginger cat had seen to that.

Margaret drank some coffee and lay down again, fighting another attack of fear and revulsion. She had always found animals unpleasant, and disgust had often made her unkind, but her terror and hatred of cats was beyond reason. Usually she knew by instinct when one was near, and took avoiding action, but when she had opened the wardrobe in room 27 and a warm streak of reddish fur had whizzed past her face into the middle of the room, she had been taken completely by surprise. Shuddering, she had grabbed the mop she used to swab the bathroom floors and as the cat, used to kindness, tried to rub itself against her ankles, had hit out at it, screaming at the pitch of her lungs.

Bruised, bleeding and yowling indignantly the cat had fled, and at once the room had been full of guests and other hotel servants, voices angrily raised.

"What's up with you, eh?"

"Are you crazy?"

"Imagine hurting Tibbles! He's a lovely cat."

"Poor pussy!"

Their contempt broke over Margaret in waves, but as she crouched sobbing against the wall she barely heard their words. Glancing up, she had caught sight of four round depressions in the ceiling seeming to mark the corners of a large square. Suddenly a warm, musty, animal smell filled her nostrils, and above the babble of voices she heard an ominous clanking of chains.

Margaret had thought then that she would never have the courage to go into room 27 again, but by next morning she had convinced herself that the previous day's experience had been a delusion caused by deep shock. She was wrong, however. When she went upstairs with her cleaning kit, the strangeness of the room continued to reveal itself.

On the surface it was just an attic bedroom, refurbished with wood-veneer furniture and draped with the hotel's ubiquitous blue and cream chintz. Not one of the Caracal's best rooms, but pleasant, with its adjoining blue bathroom and view across the river to the town. But the marks on the ceiling still troubled Margaret, and the smell that had sickened her yesterday was so strong that she couldn't understand why the room's occupants hadn't complained to Reception. She went to open the window and let in some fresh air – and that was when she noticed that the view had changed. Bewildered, she stared through the small square panes.

Trees had disappeared. The conifer hedge which screened the hotel from the road was gone, and so were the electricity pylons. Instead of factories and tower blocks Margaret could see, across a clear, unpolluted river, the frayed edges of a little market town. Patchwork gardens and narrow streets petered out into water meadows, and the cathedral rode like a huge galleon on the windy lilac sky. Perhaps the strangest thing was that momentarily this scene delighted Margaret, as if she had known it long ago but hadn't expected ever to see it again. Then down her spine she felt the familiar prickle that said, 'Cat'. She whipped round from the window but saw nothing except the rumpled bed, dirty coffee cups and yesterday's newspaper lying on the floor.

Since then the view had returned to normal, but the feeling of a cat's presence had intensified every time Margaret entered the room. She had tried to reason with herself, reminding herself that the hotel cat, nursing its wounds and being treated like a VIP in the kitchen, was as unlikely to come near her as she was to go near it. There was no other cat in the building, yet in this one room, high in the roof of Colonel Bewley's mansion, the air was unmistakably tainted with animal breath. As Margaret went about her work she sweated and whimpered with fear.

Even at home in her little flat there was no respite. Panthers and cougars prowled through her dreams and Colonel Bewley, escaped from his gilt frame in the hall, stalked them with his rifle through the trees. Waking in terror Margaret still seemed to see his lupine face, his teeth bared cruelly between thin red lips. But she had yet to recall where she had seen him before. Last night she had dreamed of a cage, suspended on chains from four hooks in the ceiling, and when in the morning she had heard in room 27 the purring of some huge unseen beast, her courage had finally deserted her. Dropping her duster she had fled weeping down the long stairs to the housekeeper's room.

"Mrs Fowler, help me! There's something awful in room 27 . . ."

Of course she hadn't been believed – and to be fair, who would believe her? Mrs Fowler, who knew about the Tibbles incident and privately wondered whether to suggest to Margaret Porter that she needed to see a doctor, had been reasonable – considering that her job was to make sure that people like Margaret did theirs.

"Go home," she had said. "Try to pull yourself together. Get a good night's sleep. You'll feel better tomorrow."

At six o'clock Margaret got up and heated some tinned soup in a pan. She poured it into a mug and as she sat drinking it, huddled over a small electric heater she felt, for the first time in a week, quite calm. Which was strange, in the circumstances. But as she had lain on her bed in the flimsy afternoon light, making a story out of her fortnight at the Caracal Hotel, something extraordinary had happened. Another story had begun to unfold itself in her mind, one which cast a lurid light on recent events but also seemed to make some sense of them. Peace like a spell had enfolded Margaret as she realised that this story was also hers. It was about another life she had lived, two hundred years ago.

Her name had been Margaret then too, but people

had called her Peg. She remembered her childhood in an orphanage in the shadow of the cathedral and how, when she was too old to live there, she had gone to work as a maidservant at Colonel Bewley's new mansion at Oman Park. That had been in 1793, just after his final return from Arabia. That was why his portrait had seemed familiar, of course. Once he had been her master.

Servants, Margaret recollected, had never stayed long at Colonel Bewley's, less because he was a foul-tempered bully than because he owned something which frightened them half to death. But she, without family or friends, had no choice. Besides, although her work was long and punishing, she had never personally been afraid.

Margaret finished her soup and strained her memory to remember the end of the story, but it was as if a dark curtain had been drawn through her mind. As she tidied up the kitchen, however, she was quite unperturbed. All last week she had gone to work at the Caracal because, a solitary orphan, she needed money; there were bills to pay and she couldn't afford to give up her job without a fight. But tomorrow she would go because someone or something from that past existence was drawing her back to room 27, eager to have her discover the end of the story. She thought she was too tired to be frightened any more. She didn't even notice that her fear of cats had completely disappeared.

Peg's mind began to take over Margaret's the moment she set foot on the attic stair. The stair was very steep and narrow, its green carpet and pink wallpaper already soiled by the passage of hotel guests and chambermaids. The old bare boards and whitewash were more practical, she thought as she toiled up with her mop and box of cleaning materials. In Colonel Bewley's day, of course, only his servants and animals had lived in this part of the house. She didn't observe that, as she emerged onto the little landing, her clumsy shoes were in fact clattering on bare boards, nor that her blue nylon overall had been replaced by a long woollen dress with a soiled scarf crossed over the chest and a filthy sacking apron. It was Peg's head she was scratching with dirty, broken fingernails, because Peg's brown hair was infested with lice.

The low, insistent growling behind the nearest door had changed to snarling as Peg's feet sounded on the landing, but she heard it with amusement. The caracal, the red-brown lynx that the Colonel had brought back from his last journey to Arabia, might bare his fangs and throw himself against the bars so that the cage juddered and the chains vibrated on their hooks, but the bolt was on the outside and he could do no harm.

Excitedly, because the impotent rage of the imprisoned beast gave her a cruel thrill, Peg opened the door and stepped into the attic room. The stench of dung and rancid meat and animal despair blasted towards her, but bad smells were everywhere and she scarcely wrinkled her nose. Through the filthy window she could glimpse the sunlit river and the little town – but her interest was in the caracal.

At her entrance the poor mad beast had stopped prowling, and stood tensing his thin back and lashing his bloodied tail. He was almost blind after more than a year in this dark, hellish place, but his scent was as keen as when he had roamed free in Arabia under a white-hot sky. And he hated the scent of Peg more than any scent on earth, even the sour smell of the evil hunter who had trapped him and brought him here in chains.

"Poor pussy!" taunted Peg as she began to torment the caracal, poking the mop handle at his soft white underparts through the massive iron bars. She had always been a cruel person, hated by the other children for her treatment of frogs and flies in the orphanage garden. To her, torturing this proud beast was no different, really, only more fun. Peg laughed as the caracal howled his anger, setting the cage swinging in his futile attempts to avoid the jabbing pole. But her laughter ceased as Margaret suddenly regained control of their shared mind – and in a belated flash of horror recollected the story's end.

Standing again in room 27 in her blue overall, Margaret remembered that, as Peg, she had always felt safe. This was because Colonel Bewley, who himself fed the animals in his horrific menagerie, was so insistent that their cage doors must be securely fastened on the outside.

"Can't have these pussies on the loose downstairs, can we?" he had barked, warning his children and servants that they must never tamper with the bolts.

The servants had been secretly exasperated. As if, they muttered to each other afterwards, anyone but a lunatic would do such a stupid thing!

Peg agreed. Which was why, on that spring morning in 1794, what had happened had filled her less with terror than with sheer surprise. For who would have imagined that as the anguished caracal hurled itself in

157

frenzy against the bars, the heavy bolt would be dislodged by the violent juddering of the cage? Silently, swiftly the door had swung open. All of this came back to Margaret in an instant before the ghostly caracal sprang.

# THE KNIGHT'S TOMB
*Michael Mullen*

"He is touched," the men said. They watched him walk down the narrow alleyway. He wore a wide-brimmed hat and a cloak. There was a scallop shell on his hat. His feet were set in old leather sandals. He appeared one evening and took up residence in the tower. Beneath the wide rim of his hat his eyes glittered. They glittered like ruby stones. He spoke gibberish. At least it appeared to be gibberish.

Sometimes he stopped before the trench and called out loudly. He crossed himself and put his hands to his eyes as if to ward off some evil sight. He never left the old section of the city. Each day he passed by the workers. He noted their progress. Each day they removed a layer of earth from the site. The hollow grew deeper.

They had passed down into the foundations of the old medieval city. The earth was black and sterile.

The archaeologist was with them. He had mapped out a section of the plot. Now with brushes and trowels they had descended into the trench and began the

159

meticulous work.

The strange figure appeared. He crossed himself and called out something. He repeated the same words again and again.

"Away with you," one of the men said. "You are a fool. You disturb our work."

The archaeologist looked at the figure. He spoke to him in a strange tongue. He was a burly man from the museum who had worked on several excavations in Southern France and the Near East. He was an expert in his field.

"What language did you speak?" they asked when the man had passed down through one of the alleys.

"It is a strange language from Southern France."

"How are you acquainted with it?"

"I worked for a while in Languedoc."

"And what did he say?" they asked looking at each other. For a moment they were afraid. A cold chill passed down their backs.

"Nothing of importance," the archaeologist said.

"It must have been something of importance. Perhaps we should know. You must tell us, otherwise we will abandon the dig."

"Very well. He said something about a Knight's tomb."

"And what did he say about the Knight's tomb?"

"Nothing. He just mentioned the Knight's tomb. He believes that we will soon reach it."

"How does he know these things?"

"He is both Jew and Gentile. He belongs to a world that passed five hundred years ago. He is a pilgrim and travels from shrine to shrine."

"There is no shrine here," one replied.

"Once upon a time there was."

The men seemed hesitant. They had never been happy about the dig. From the beginning it had been dogged with bad luck. A piece of masonry had dislodged from the wall and crushed one of their friends. Another had gone down with a mysterious chill. His skin had turned yellow and beads of icy cold sweat formed on his face. When they touched his body it was as cold as a corpse. Something was drawing the life force from it. And now the madman had called out in some foreign tongue which made sense to the archaeologist. Something was wrong and they could not put their finger on it.

It was a hot summer's day. The sky was clear and blue, yet the wind which blew through the old town was chilly. They continued the dig. It was boring work. They brushed up the surface dust and examined it for ancient remains. If they found nothing they dumped it in a skip. Then they dug the next layer of earth and studied it. After three hours work they had recovered nothing of any importance.

"There is nothing here," they told the archaeologist.

"It is not your business to question my decisions," he said curtly.

They disliked him. He had a rutted face and leathery skin from work in the open. He never smiled or spoke a kind word. His mind was harsh. At dinner time they sat about and talked. They could not define their fear.

"There is evil lurking somewhere. It's in the ground. It's in the walls. The further we go down the more sinister it gets. The earth seems poisoned," one said.

Later, they returned reluctantly to their work. They kept digging. The soil was free and yielded nothing of importance. The sun began to cast shadows into the trench.

"Why does the pilgrim fear this plot?" one of the workers asked.

"Perhaps because it is in unconsecrated ground and he is superstitious," the archaeologist said.

"And how do you know that it is unconsecrated?" they asked.

"We have an old map of the area. The site is marked."

"So the Knight, if he is here, was a heretic or did some terrible deed?"

"Perhaps. There could be other reasons, of course. It was all such a long time ago."

Then they reached a solid slab of rock at the left side of the site. The archaeologist quickly descended into the trench. He cleared away the upper part. There was an inscription in Latin.

"I knew it was here all the time," he said. "I knew it was here!"

He spoke excitedly as he cleared away more of the black earth. He exposed the upper part of a slab of limestone. They watched him clear off the grime from further lettering.

"What does it say?" they asked. "What does it say?"

"'The Final Knight Rests Here'. That is all," he told them.

"What does that mean?" they inquired.

"Nothing. It means nothing."

But they were suspicious. He was not telling them

the truth. He thought they were fools who did not understand old matters.

"What will you do with the tomb?" they asked him.

"Tomorrow I will open it."

"Why not leave the dead rest?"

"It must be opened. The Knight is not dead. He is half dead." The words had escaped from his mouth before he realised what he had spoken.

"Half dead. What do you mean?"

"Nothing. I refer to an old medieval belief."

They looked at each other. They disliked the archaeologist. They had disliked him from the very beginning. His eyes were the eyes of a maniac. For no reason a wind blew up from nowhere. It cried through the lanes. They felt cold again.

"It is the tomb. We should not tamper with the tomb," they said.

"It is nothing," the archaeologist replied. "A freak wind."

They put their tools in the small site shed and locked the door. They said good evening to the archaeologist but he did not hear them. He was kneeling on the tombstone, running his finger along a strange geometric pattern which he had uncovered.

They sat in the tavern. It had originally been a cellar and they retired there each evening. It was close to the site and part of the old city.

"That's strange," the owner said when he served them.

"What's strange?" they asked.

"The ceiling. It is weeping." He ran his fingers along the vault. There was a coat of white on the surface. "It is as cold as ice," he remarked.

"When did it start to weep?" they asked.

"Two hours ago. Why do you ask?"

"No reason. No reason at all," they replied. They looked at each other knowingly.

"I don't like it. I don't like it at all. There is more here than meets the eye. And I don't believe that he gave us the full translation. Did you see the look on his face as he revealed the inscriptions? It was transfixed," one of the men said.

They wondered if they should return to the site on the morrow.

As they prepared to depart one said, "There is something evil in that tomb. It should not be opened. The dead should be left undisturbed."

"But he said the 'half dead'. What did he mean by 'half dead'?"

Unresolved questions troubled their minds.

Meanwhile, the archaeologist had taken a lantern and set it beside him on the slab. He took some drawings from his pocket and compared them with those on the tomb. Yes. He was right. This was the tomb of the third Knight. He would be wealthy beyond his wildest dreams. Beneath him, around the Knight's neck, lay the Golden Obelisk. It carried the codes which would lead him to the Treasures of the Temple. He would return to Jerusalem. Somewhere beneath the city, in the dark bowels of the earth, lay vast treasures.

It began to grow dark. He continued to expose the great slab which covered the tomb. It was exactly like the others. It possessed the same markings, the same codes. He was drawing close to the end of the mystery.

The golden obelisk would fit in the door with the others. Then it would swing open. And beyond the door lay power and glory.

He decided to open the tomb. The place was empty. He took a strong steel wire and secured it to the top of the slab. Then he started the small excavator on the edge of the dig. The arm stiffened. The wire became taut. He began to draw up the arm. The arc of light shone directly into the trench. The slab began to move very slowly.

From beneath the slab they came: dark insects which had shunned the light for five hundred years. They clustered together like some evil brain. They passed into the old quarter of the town.

For a moment the archaeologist hesitated. Had he released the old evil? Would the Grey Death stalk the town? He did not care. He drew up the slab. It rose to a steep angle. Instantly the archaeologist jumped from the seat of the excavator. He slid down into the trench. He took the lamp and shone it inside.

He screamed. It was a wild scream which cut the night. The Knight was alive. His eyes gleamed like live embers. Clasped in his joined hands lay the golden obelisk.

The Knight stared at the archaeologist. There was a grim look on his face. Then he began to rot. A stench rose from his body. His flesh turned green. It began to disintegrate. The knuckle bones appeared.

"It's mine, mine!" the archaeologist cried as he grabbed at the golden obelisk. He tried to wrest it from the skeletal hands.

Suddenly the Knight sprang forward. He plunged the

golden obelisk into the archaeologist's chest. He gasped his last breath. The golden obelisk was lodged in his chest.

The Knight laughed eerily. The archaeologist fell forward on to the rotting body. The Knight pushed him aside and rose out of the tomb – a skeleton dressed in old armour. His eyes glowed and cast a red radiance about him. He climbed up from the tomb and began to walk through the old part of the city, uttering deep throaty sounds. It seemed that the words were coming from some dark empty cave. His armour clanged.

The men emerged from the tavern. It was half dark in the alley way. They heard the strange buzzing of insects. As they made their way down the alley they were attacked. The evil mass descended upon them and covered their faces like a mask. They cried out at the savage bites.

Then the insects disappeared.

They looked at each other. Strange blisters appeared on their faces. They rushed down the street. When they reached the end of the old town they found they could not pass out of it. It appeared that a glass wall had been built about it. They pushed and tore at the invisible wall. Now their bodies were parched. They were burning with fever. They cried out for water.

"Save us," they called. "Bring us water!"

But their voices did not pass through the invisible wall.

The insects entered all the rooms of the old quarter. Soon a plague raged amongst the people. They caught their parched throats and ran out on to the streets.

All except the pilgrim. He knew what to expect. He

had waited for them. He knew their sinister power. They buzzed about the windows.

"The old enemy. I know you. You will not rise against us."

He lit the candles on the menorah. The seven candles burned steadily. They gave off a sweet incense. In a circle in the centre of the floor other candles burned. He stood amongst them. Then, with a snap of a leather thong, he opened the window. A dust cloud of insects poured through. Their hum was poisonous. In the light it rose up several pitches. The evil within them was angry.

The pilgrim called out an old Hebrew Prayer. The pitch grew sharp and venomous. Then they rushed towards the menorah and were burned on the sacred flames.

"I have waited for this," the old man said as he left the circle of light. "I have now to ease a tormented soul."

He took his staff and passed down the stone steps of the towers. He passed through those who lay stretched on the street crying out for water. And then he discovered the Knight. His flesh had fallen from his body and he was white-boned. Only the red eyes gleamed. He called out in a dry tone which only the pilgrim could understand.

"Save me. Save me. I thirst. I walk in lonely places. None will speak to me."

"You have desecrated the temple treasures."

"I did evil deeds. I killed the others. They are all dead in the treasure chamber."

"Except me," the pilgrim said. "I escaped. I had come

to bless the treasures. You had come to steal them. You and your friends."

"Father Alcuin, is it you?"

"Yes."

"And you too live."

"I come to lead you back to a restful place where you will have no further torment. You once gave water to a beggar. It has stood to you."

"Water to a beggar. I have forgotten. It was a small thing."

"It weighed in the balance."

"A drop of water?"

"One drop of water. Follow me. I can walk on sanctified ground."

They passed through the old city. They came to the great abbey with its ruined choir. The pilgrim opened the door. It creaked.

"Follow me."

"I am afraid. I have desecrated sacred places."

"There is no need to be afraid."

The Knight entered the great church. It seemed to glow with mysterious light.

"How wonderful light is," he said. "I have moved in the regions of darkness peopled by grey creatures."

"Come with me. A place has been prepared."

The crypt was open. They moved down the spiral stairs.

Lying in the centre, with a slab to one side was an empty tomb.

"I have sought rest here for a long time. I knew I could not enter."

The Knight passed down into the tomb. The pilgrim,

with some supernatural strength, drew the stone over him.

"You are no longer the living dead," he said.

He left the great abbey church and returned to his tower. All that night he cried out in Hebrew that the sun might rise over the old part of the town and bring a fresh beginning.

Then as the light poured through the streets people began to stir from their fevered sleep. They could not account for what had happened to them.

The workers who had fallen at the invisible wall shook themselves. "We must return to the site quickly," they said. When they returned they noted that the lid of the tomb had been slightly moved.

"Leave it be. Cover it up," the foreman directed.

Quickly the trench was filled with earth. They did not know that the body of the archaeologist, with the golden obelisk lodged deep in his chest, was buried underneath. Then they pushed an old wall on to the site.

When they were finished the pilgrim passed down the narrow alleyway. He was carrying his staff. There seemed to be a spring in his step. They watched him pass. He seemed to have grown younger. He passed out of the old city. Then he disappeared.

Other books in **Poolbeg's**
Fantasy list for you to enjoy!

*Chiller*
ISBN: 1-85371-512-3

*Nightmares*
ISBN: 1-85371-629-4

*She Fades Away* by Michael Carroll
ISBN: 1-85371-621-9

*Cold Places* by Morgan Llywelyn
ISBN: 1-85371-541-7

*19 Railway Street* by Scott/Llywelyn
ISBN: 1-85371-642-1

*Vampyre* by Michael Scott
ISBN: 1-85371-545-X

*Blood Brother* by JH Brennan
ISBN: 1-85371-602-2